How to Steal a Dog

Also by Barbara O'Connor

BARBARA O'CONNOR

How to Steal a Dog

SQUARE
FISH

FARRAR STRAUS GIROUX

New York

SQUARE FISH

An Imprint of Macmillan Publishing Group, LLC

HOW TO STEAL A DOG. Copyright © 2007 by Barbara O'Connor.
All rights reserved. Printed in the United States of America
by LSC Communications, Harrisonburg, Virginia.
For information, address Square Fish, 175 Fifth Avenue,
New York, NY 10010.

Square Fish and the Square Fish logo are trademarks of Macmillan
and are used by Farrar Straus Giroux under license from Macmillan.

Library of Congress Cataloging-in-Publication Data
O'Connor, Barbara.
  How to steal a dog / Barbara O'Connor.
    p. cm.
  Summary: Living in the family car in their small North Carolina town after their father leaves them virtually penniless, Georgina, desperate to
  improve their situation and unwilling to accept her overworked mother's calls for patience, persuades her younger brother to help her in an
  elaborate scheme to get money by stealing a dog and then claiming the
  reward that the owners are bound to offer.
  ISBN 978-0-312-56112-3
  [I. Homeless persons—Fiction. 2. Family problems—Fiction.
  3. Conduct of life—Fiction. 4. Interpersonal relations—Fiction.
  5. Brothers and sisters—Fiction. 6. Dogs—Fiction. 7. North
  Carolina—Fiction.] I. Title.

PZ7.O217 How 2007
[Fic]—dc22

2005040166

Originally published in the United States by Farrar Straus Giroux
Square Fish logo designed by Filomena Tuosto
Designed by Aimee Fleck

First Square Fish Edition: April 2009
27   29   30   28
mackids.com

AR: 4.0 / F&P: T / LEXILE: 700L

To the dogs in my life:

Phoebe, the sweet one
Matty, the angry one
And Murphy, the one who stole my heart

How To Steal a Dog

1

The day I decided to steal a dog was the same day my best friend, Luanne Godfrey, found out I lived in a car.

I had told Mama she would find out sooner or later, seeing as how she's so nosy and all. But Mama had rolled her eyes and said, "Just get on up there to the bus stop, Georgina, and quit your whining."

So that's what I did. I stood up there at the bus stop pretending like I still lived in Apartment 3B. I pretended like I didn't have mustard on my shirt from the day before. I pretended like I hadn't washed my hair in the bathroom of the Texaco gas station that very morning. And I pretended like my daddy hadn't just waltzed off and left us with nothing but three rolls of quarters and a mayonnaise jar full of wadded-up dollar bills.

I guess I'm pretty good at pretending.

My brother, Toby, however, is not so good at pretending. When Mama told him to get on up to the bus stop and quit his whining, he cried and carried on like the baby that he is.

"What's wrong with Toby?" Luanne asked me when we were standing at the bus stop.

"He has an earache," I said, trying as hard as anything to look like my life was just as normal as could be instead of all crazy like it really was.

When I saw Luanne's eyes narrow and her lips squeeze together, I knew her nosiness was about to irritate me.

Sure enough, she said, "Then how come your mama is making him go to school?" She kept looking at me with that squinty-eyed look of hers, but I didn't let on that I was irritated. I just shrugged and hoped she would hush up about Toby.

She did. But then she went and turned her nosy self loose on me.

"No offense, Georgina," she said. "But you're starting to look kind of unkempt."

Unkempt? That was her mama talking if I'd ever heard it. Luanne wouldn't never have said that word "unkempt" if she hadn't heard her mama say it first.

And what was I supposed to say to that anyways? Was I supposed to say, "Well, for your information, Luanne Godfrey, it's kinda hard to keep your clothes looking nice when you've been sleeping in the backseat of a Chevrolet for a week"?

Or maybe I was supposed to say, "I know it, Luanne. But my hairbrush got tossed out in that pile of stuff Mr.

Deeter left on the sidewalk when he kicked us out of our apartment."

And then Luanne would say, "Why'd Mr. Deeter do that?"

And I would say, " 'Cause three rolls of quarters and a mayonnaise jar full of wadded-up dollar bills doesn't pay the rent, Luanne."

But I didn't say anything. I acted like I hadn't heard that word "unkempt." I just climbed on the bus and sat in the sixth seat on the left side with Luanne, like I always did.

I knew Luanne wouldn't give up, though. I knew she'd keep on till she found out the truth.

"What if she wants to come over?" I said to Mama. "Or what if she looks in the window or something and finds out we don't live there anymore?"

But Mama just flapped her hand at me and closed her eyes to let me know how tired she was from working two jobs. So every day I imagined Luanne peeking in the kitchen window of Apartment 3B. When she did, of course, she wouldn't see me and Toby and Mama and Daddy eating our dinner and being happy. She'd see some other family. Some happy family that wasn't all broken up like mine.

And then one day, when we got off the school bus,

Luanne went and did the nosiest thing I could imagine. She *followed* me. I was trying to catch up with Toby 'cause he had grabbed the car key and run on ahead of me, so I didn't even notice her sneaking along behind me. She followed me all the way past Apartment 3B, across the street, and clear on around the back of Eckerd Drugstore, where our car was parked with laundry hanging out the windows and Toby sitting on a milk crate waiting for me.

If there was ever a time when I wished the earth would open up and swallow me whole, it was when I turned around and saw Luanne looking at me and Toby and that car and all. I could see her thoughts just plain as day right there on her face.

I wanted to wave my hand and make that dented-up car disappear off the face of the earth. But more than anything, I wanted my daddy to come on home and change everything back to the way it was before.

I set a smile on my face and said, "It's just temporary," like Mama had said to me about a hundred times.

Luanne turned red and said, "Oh."

"When Mama gets paid, we're moving into our new apartment," I said.

"Oh."

And then we both just stood there, looking at our feet. I could feel the distance between us grow and grow until it seemed like Luanne Godfrey, who had been my friend forever, was standing clear on the other side of the universe from me.

Finally, she said, "I better go."

But she didn't. She just stood there and I squeezed my eyes shut and told myself not to look pitiful and, for heaven's sake, don't cry.

And then, of course, Toby had to go and make everything worse by saying, "Mama left a note that she's working late, so we're supposed to eat that macaroni that's in the cooler."

Luanne arched her eyebrows up and then she said, "I haven't seen your daddy in a long time."

That did it. I couldn't stop the tears from spilling out of my squeezed-up eyes. I sat down right there in the drugstore parking lot and told Luanne everything.

I felt her arm around me and I heard her saying something, but I was too lost in my misery to do anything but cry. When I was all cried out, I stood up and brushed the dirt off the seat of my pants, pushed the hair out of my eyes, and said, "Promise you won't tell?"

Luanne nodded. "I promise."

"I mean, not even your mama."

Luanne's eyes flickered for just a second, but then she said, "Okay."

I crooked my pinkie finger in the air and waited for her to give me the pinkie promise, but she hesitated.

I stamped my foot and jabbed my pinkie at her. Finally she crooked her pinkie around mine and we shook.

"I better go," she said.

I watched her hurry across the parking lot, then glance back at me before disappearing around the corner of the drugstore.

"I hate that macaroni," Toby said from his seat on the milk crate. It was just like him to not even give me one little minute to wallow in my misery.

I stomped around to the back of the car and kicked the cooler, sending it toppling over on its side. Ice and water and plastic containers spilled out onto the parking lot.

"Me too," I said.

Then I climbed into the backseat of the car and waited for Mama to come back.

It was way past dark when I heard Mama's shoes click-clacking on the asphalt as she made her way toward the car. I sat up and looked out the window. Even in the dim glow of the streetlights, I could see her tired, sad look. Part of me wanted to stay put and just go on back to sleep and leave her be, but another part of me wanted to get out and have my say, which is what I did.

Mama jumped when I opened the car door.

"What in the world are you doing awake, Georgina?" she said.

"I hate this," I said. "I don't want to do this anymore."

I pushed the car door shut softly so Toby wouldn't wake up; then I turned back to Mama and said, "You got to do something. You got to find us a place to live. A *real* place. Not a car."

Mama reached out like she was gonna touch me, so I jerked away. She dropped her hand to her side like it was heavy as cement. Then she let out a whoosh of breath that blew her hair up off her forehead.

"I'm trying," she said.

"*How* are you trying?"

She tossed her purse through the car window into the front seat. "I just am, okay, Georgina?"

"But how?"

"I'm working two jobs. What else do you want me to do?"

"Find us a place to live." I stomped away from her and then whirled back around. "This is all your fault."

She stormed over and grabbed me by the shoulders.

"It takes *money* to get a place." She gave me a little shake when she said the word "money."

"I'm trying to save up, okay?" she said.

She let go of me and leaned against the car.

"How much money do we need?" I said.

She looked up at the sky like the answer was written up there in the stars. Then she shook her head real slow and said, "I don't know, Georgina. A lot, okay?"

"Like how much?"

"More than we got."

We both just stood there in the dark and listened to the crickets from the vacant lot next door.

Mama draped her arm around my shoulder, and I laid my head against her and wanted to be a baby again—a baby that just cries and then gets taken care of and that's all there is to a day.

Finally I asked her the same question I'd asked her about a million times already.

"Why did Daddy leave?"

I felt her whole body go limp. "I wish I knew." She brushed my hair out of my eyes. "Just got tired of it all, I reckon," she said.

"Tired of what?"

The silence between us felt big and dark, like a wall. Then I asked her the question that had been burning a hole in my heart. "Tired of me?"

Mama took my chin in her hand and looked at me hard. "This is not your fault, okay?"

She peered inside the car at Toby, all curled up in a ball in the backseat.

"We got to go," she said.

"Where?"

"I don't know. Just somewhere else." The car door creaked when she opened it, sending an echo into the still night air. "We've been here two nights now," she said. "The cops are liable to run us off if we don't leave."

She shot me a look when she saw the overturned cooler, so I helped her gather things up before I climbed back in the car. As we drove out of the parking lot, I slouched down and stared glumly out the window. The empty shops we passed made Darby, North Carolina, seem like a ghost town, all locked up and dark.

Mama pulled the car into the alley beside Bill's Auto Parts. When she shut the engine off, we got swallowed up in quiet.

I draped a beach towel over the clothesline that Mama had strung along the middle of the car to make me a bedroom. I could picture Luanne, snuggled in her pink-and-white quilt with her stuffed animals lined up along the wall beside her and her gymnastics ribbons taped on her headboard, and I sure felt sorry for myself.

Then I curled up on the seat, turning every which way trying to get comfortable. Finally I settled on my back with my feet propped against the car door and stared out at the starry sky.

And then I saw it. A sign, tacked up there on a telephone pole right outside the car window. A faded old sign that said: REWARD. $500. And under that was a picture of a bug-eyed little dog with its tongue hanging out.

And then under that it said: HAVE YOU SEEN ME? MY NAME IS MITSY.

Five hundred dollars! Who in the world would pay five hundred dollars for that little ole dog?

"Mama?" I whispered through my beach towel wall.

Mama rustled some in the front seat.

"Would five hundred dollars be enough money to get us a place to live?" I said.

Mama sighed. "I suppose so, Georgina. Now go to sleep. You got school tomorrow."

I looked up at Mitsy and my mind started churning.

What if I could find that dog? I could get that money, and we could have a real place to live instead of this stinking old car.

But that dog could be anywhere. I wouldn't even know where to look. Besides, that sign was old. Somebody had probably already found Mitsy and got that five hundred dollars.

I stared out the window at the sign, thinking about Mitsy and wondering if there were other folks out there who would pay money for their lost dogs.

And that's when I got a thought that made me sit up so fast Toby mumbled in his sleep and Mama hissed, "Shhhh."

I folded my legs up and lay back down in my beach towel bedroom. The damp car seat smelled like greasy french fries and bug spray. I closed my eyes and smiled to myself. I had a plan.

I was gonna steal me a dog.

2

I thought about my plan for a couple of days before I decided to tell Toby. "You got to keep this a secret," I told him.

I glanced out the back window of the car, then pulled the beach towel over our heads. Mama had left for work, and me and Toby were waiting till it was time to walk up to the bus stop.

Toby nodded in the darkness under the towel. "I will," he said.

I pushed my face up closer to his and said, "You can't tell *anybody*, okay?"

"Okay."

I knew it was risky telling Toby my plan, but I figured I had to. Mama said he had to stay with me after school, so there I was, stuck with him. I couldn't even go to Luanne's or anything. How was I gonna steal a dog without Toby finding out? Then he'd go and tell Mama, for sure. If I made him think he was part of my secret plan, maybe he wouldn't be the tattletale baby that he usually is.

"Here's my plan," I said.

I paused a minute to add some drama 'cause Toby likes drama. He stared at me with wide eyes. His breath smelled like tuna fish, and I was wishing I hadn't covered us up with the towel like that.

"We're gonna steal a dog," I said. "How about *that*?" I grinned and waited for him to say "Hot dang" like he does, but he just stared at me with his mouth hanging open. That tuna fish odor swirled around us inside our beach towel tent. I waved my hand in front of my nose and flipped the towel off of us.

"Jeez, Toby," I said. "Can't you brush your teeth?"

He glared at me. "How?" he hollered. "There ain't no sink in here." He waved his arms around the car.

"Use the water in the cooler," I said.

"No way. It's cruddy."

"Well, anyways," I said. "Don't you want to know *why* we're gonna steal a dog?"

He nodded, sending a clump of greasy hair flopping down over his eyes. He had Mama's straight, copper-colored hair, but I had to go and get Daddy's curly ole black hair that I hate. One more good reason to be mad at my daddy.

I smoothed the crumpled yellowing sign out on the seat between us. "Because of *this*," I said.

Toby looked at it. "What's it say?"

"For crying out loud, Toby, you're in third grade." I jabbed a finger at the sign. "*Reward*, it says. Five hundred dollars reward for this ugly ole dog. Can you believe that?"

"He's not ugly."

"*She*," I said. "Her name is Mitsy. See?" I jabbed at the sign again.

Toby squeezed his eyebrows together. "Why are we gonna steal that dog?"

"Not *this* dog, you idiot," I said. "We're gonna steal a *different* dog."

"What dog?"

"I don't know yet," I said. "That's why I need you to help me."

I looked out the window again. The alley beside the auto parts store was empty. I slouched down lower in the seat and motioned for Toby to come closer.

"Listen," I whispered. "We're gonna find us a dog that somebody loves so much, they'd pay a reward to get it back." I poked Toby with my elbow. "Get it?"

"Pay a reward to who?" Toby said.

I sighed and shook my head. "To *us*, you ninny."

"But why would they pay us if we steal their dog?"

I rolled my eyes and flopped back against the seat.

"I swear, Toby, sometimes I wonder about you." I sat back up and took him by the shoulders, looking him square in the eyes. "The person who loves the dog won't *know* it was us that stole it. The person will think we *found* the dog. *Now* do you get it?"

Toby grinned. "Okay," he said. "Where's the dog?"

"We've got to *find* the dog," I hollered.

I slapped my hand over my mouth and glanced quickly around us. The alley was still empty.

"We've got to *find* the dog," I repeated in a whisper. "Mama said five hundred dollars is enough to get a place to live. If we steal a dog, we can get five hundred dollars, see?"

Toby had a look on his face that made me think I'd made a mistake sharing my plan with him.

"Listen, Toby," I said. "It's the only way we're ever gonna have us a real place to live instead of this car, you hear?"

He nodded.

"Don't you want a real place to live?"

He nodded again.

"Then we got to steal us a dog and get the reward," I said. "And if you tell anyone, and I mean *anyone*, you might as well just say your prayers and kiss this earth goodbye, you hear me?"

"Okay," he said. "But how do we steal a dog?"

"Don't worry," I said. "I'm working on it."

After school that day, me and Toby raced back to the car. When I unlocked it, Toby climbed in the driver's seat and started spreading peanut butter on a saltine cracker with his finger. I climbed in the backseat and locked the doors. Mama had told us to stay put. If anybody asked us what we were doing, we were supposed to say we were waiting for our mama, who was in the bank next door.

I rummaged through my trash bag of stuff. When I found my spiral notebook with the glittery purple cover, I opened it to a fresh page and wrote:

How to Steal a Dog
by
Georgina Hayes

I wrote the date in the margin: *April 5*. Then, next to that, I wrote:

Step 1: Find a Dog.

I chewed on the end of my pencil and looked out the window. Someone came out of the side door of the auto parts store and threw a cardboard box in the Dumpster. I slouched down real quick and waited till I heard the shop door slam shut. Then I wrote:

These are the rules for finding a dog:
1. The dog must not bark too much.
2. The dog must not bite.
3. The dog must be outside by itself sometimes.
4. The dog must be loved a lot and not just some old dog that nobody cares about.
5. The owner of the dog must look like somebody who will

pay a lot of money to get their dog back, like maybe someone who has a big house and rides in a limo or something like that.

But then I scratched out that part about the limo 'cause who ever saw a limo in Darby, North Carolina?

I chewed my pencil some more and looked up at the top of the car. Dark brown stains formed patterns like clouds up there. Over the driver's side, Mama had used safety pins to put up phone numbers for me and Toby in case we needed somebody. I guess she forgot we didn't have a phone in that stinking car.

As I read my list of rules over again, I felt myself splitting right in two. Half of me was thinking, *Georgina, don't do this. Stealing a dog is just plain wrong.*

The other half of me was thinking, *Georgina, you're in a bad fix and you got to do whatever it takes to get yourself out of it.*

I sat there in that car feeling myself get yanked one way and then the other. So I just made myself stop thinking, and I read those rules one more time.

I was pretty sure I had covered everything. I stuffed my notebook way down in the bottom of my bag and said, "Come on, Toby. Let's go find us a dog."

3

O kay," I said to Toby. "You go that way and I'll go this way."

He squinted in the direction I had pointed.

"I don't see no dogs down there," he said.

I sighed. Maybe I should've asked Luanne to help me. I wanted to, but I just had this feeling she would mess things up worse than Toby was liable to. Not on purpose, but she just would. Mainly because of her mama, who finds out everything we do even if Luanne doesn't tell. And Mrs. Godfrey doesn't like me one little bit. She pinches her face up real hateful-like when I go over there. One time I saw her wiping off Luanne's bedroom door with a sponge right where I had touched it. Like I had left my cooties there to infect her family. And when I used to invite Luanne over to my apartment, her mama would always find a reason to say no. She could pluck a reason out of the air like a magician plucks a rabbit out of his hat. A dentist appointment. A visiting relative. A sudden need to shop for new shoes.

So I knew asking Luanne to help me steal a dog

would probably be a bad idea. But Toby? I could see he was gonna be more trouble than help. But what choice did I have?

"Listen, Toby," I said real slow and calm. "You got to walk down there and *look*. Look in the yards. Look on the porches. Look in the *back*yards, even. Just look, okay?"

He nodded. "Okay." He started off down the street, then stopped. "What do I do if I see one?"

"Come get me."

"Okay."

"And remember the rules for the dogs," I said. "You know, about not barking and all that? Okay?"

"Okay."

We went in opposite directions. The first dog I saw came trotting right up the street toward me. He was brown with tufts of fur that stuck together in clumps. Every few feet, he stopped to sniff the ground.

"Hey, boy," I called to him.

He looked up and wagged his scrawny tail. His face had bald spots on it. One eye was closed up into a slit with gnats swarming all around it. Nope, that dog wouldn't do. Nobody cared about *him*, that was for sure.

I gave him a little pat on the head 'cause I felt sorry for him, then continued on down the street. When I came to a house with a trailer beside it, a dog started barking. A shrill, yipping bark. When I got closer, I saw a dog tied to a clothesline on the side of the house.

A short-legged dog with a smooshed-in nose and a curlicue tail. When he saw me, he raced back and forth along the clothesline, his yippy bark getting shriller and shriller.

From inside the trailer, a man's voice hollered, "Shut up, Sparky!"

Nope. That dog wouldn't do, either. Too noisy.

A few houses farther on, a great big dog with bushy black fur sat by the side of the road watching me. When I tried to pet him, he slinked away with his tail between his legs. Then some woman came out with a rolled-up newspaper. She smacked him on the rear, hauled him off by the collar, and pushed him up under the porch.

"Get under there like I told you," she said.

Then she stomped back up the steps and went inside. She didn't seem like someone who would pay money for her dog.

Finally, at the end of the street, I saw a dog who had *steal me* written all over him. He was clean and fluffy with a red bandanna tied around his neck. He didn't bark when I got closer. He even let me pet him, wagging his tail like he was the happiest dog on earth. I was about to think I'd found the perfect dog to steal, but then I took one look at his house and I changed my mind. The front steps were rotted right off the porch, lying in a heap of lumber in the red-dirt yard. Bricks and boards were stacked to make steps into the tiny house with its peeling paint and torn screens. A plastic window box had come loose on one side, spilling dirt and dried-up brown flowers into the bushes. A rusty old car sat on cinder blocks in the gravel driveway.

Nope. That dog wouldn't do, either. The people in that house weren't rich. I bet they'd never pay five hundred dollars for their dog, no matter how much they loved it.

It looked like it was going to be harder than I thought to find a dog that fit all the rules in my notebook.

I crossed over to the corner and waited for Toby. When I saw him skipping up the road toward me, I called out, "Any luck?"

"I only saw one, and he growled at me."

"Only one? Are you sure?"

"I saw some cats."

"No, cats won't do."

"How come?"

"They just won't," I said. "Let's try one more street. Then we gotta get on back to the car before Mama gets off work."

I hurried over to the next block. Toby kept stopping to pick stuff up along the side of the road. Rocks and acorns and wrappers and things. I had to go back and yank him a couple of times. When we got to the corner, I looked at the street sign. Whitmore Road.

"This one looks good," I said. "Let's go up one side and down the other. You stay with me."

We walked along the street, peering over fences, sneaking into backyards. No luck.

Suddenly Toby pointed. "Look at *that* house," he said.

Just ahead of us was a huge brick house set back off the street a ways. All the other houses on that street were small, one-story, wooden houses with tiny yards and no porches. But that brick house was two stories high. I bet it had a whole bunch of rooms inside.

"Come on," I said to Toby, "let's go check it out."

We ran to the house. It towered over the little houses next to it. The front yard was the biggest one on the whole street, with a chain-link fence all the way around it. Along the fence was a thick hedge taller than me.

I peered over the gate. That house looked like a mansion. It had a front porch with rocking chairs and a swing painted the same color green as the shutters on the windows. In the yard, there were flowers everywhere, popping up between the bushes, curling around the lamppost, blooming in pots on the front steps.

And then I couldn't hardly believe my eyes. There in the bushes along the porch was a dog. A little black-and-white dog digging so hard that dirt was flying out behind him. His rear end was stuck up in the air and his scraggly tail was wagging away while his front legs worked faster and faster at the dirt.

Then a voice came through the screen door.

"Willy!" A big, fat woman came out onto the porch.

I ducked behind the hedge and pulled Toby down beside me. I put my finger to my lips and said, "Shhhh."

I waited to hear her holler mean things at that dog for digging up the yard. Then I bet she was gonna come storming off the porch and smack him. But she didn't holler. She laughed! Then she said, "What am I gonna do with you, you naughty little thing?"

I crawled on my hands and knees and peeked through the gate.

The woman was sitting on the porch steps, holding the little dog in her lap and letting him lick her all over her face. When she scratched him up and down his back, he stuck his face in the air, closed his eyes, and kicked one leg, leaving streaks of mud all over her shorts. She took his head in both her hands and rubbed her nose back and forth against his nose. Like the Eskimo kisses my daddy used to give me a long time ago when he loved me.

Then she picked the dog up and went inside.

My insides were getting all swirled around with excitement while I went over the dog-stealing rules in my head. I mentally checked them off one by one. That little dog didn't look like he'd bite a flea. He didn't bark one bit. And it was for sure that dog was loved.

I glanced at the house again. That was one big house. That lady *must* be rich. Then, as if I needed one more thing to convince me, something caught my attention. The mailbox next to the gate was kind of rusty and leaning over just a tad, but it had big black letters painted on the side of it that said: THE WHITMORES. Whitmores? That lady was named Whitmore and this was Whitmore Road.

"Toby!" I said. "That lady *owns* this whole street! Can you believe that?"

His eyes grew big and he shook his head.

I grinned and gave him a thumbs-up.

"Toby," I said, "I think we just found us a dog."

4

I sat in the car behind the steering wheel and turned the envelope over and over. I read the messy handwriting scrawled across the front. *Mr. and Mrs. Hayes.*

I put it up to my nose and sniffed. I could actually smell my teacher, Mr. White. Sort of like soap and toothpaste and coffee all mixed together. I pressed the envelope against the window and tried to read the letter inside. I turned it every which way, but I couldn't make out a single word.

I was pretty sure I knew what it said, though. Stuff about me. About the homework I hadn't done and the math test I had failed. Probably even about how ugly I looked all the time now, with my wrinkled clothes and my dirty hair. And why was I so sleepy every day? And sometimes I didn't have lunch money. I bet the letter said how Mr. White had tried to call Mama but our phone didn't work. I bet the letter said all that stuff.

I rolled the window down and looked out at the weeds beside the road. It was only April, but it was already beginning to feel like summer. Lucky for us the nights were still cool, though, 'cause Mama made us keep the windows rolled up all night long. She said it was because she hated bugs and flies and things getting in the car, but I think it was because she thought some bad guy might reach his hand in.

I had been glad when Mama said Toby was going to go to work with her that afternoon. But now I was bored. I guess I should've gone on over to Luanne's like I said I was.

I could hear kids over in the school playground. I wished Mama hadn't parked the car so close to school. What if someone I knew saw me sitting there? What would I say? Besides, I didn't see why we had to keep moving around so much. After two nights in the same place, off we went, to some new spot. Now we were parked too close to school and farther away from Whitmore Road. How was I supposed to keep an eye on that dog if we kept parking so far away?

I climbed into the backseat and stuffed the envelope from Mr. White way down inside my trash bag of stuff. Then I pulled out my notebook and turned to the page that said:

How to Steal a Dog
by
Georgina Hayes

I wrote *April 6* in the margin. Then, after *Step 1*, I skipped two lines and wrote:

Step 2: When you find the dog you want to steal, keep an eye on it for a while. Here are the rules to remember:

1. Make sure the dog really doesn't bark or bite.

2. If there is a fence, see if the gate is locked.

3. Decide whether or not you can pick the dog up or maybe you have to have a leash or a rope.

4. Check to see if there are any nosy people living next door or across the street or something.

I closed my notebook, climbed out of the car, and locked the door with the key I wore around my neck. Then I set off for Whitmore Road.

When I got there, I stopped for a minute to check things out. The street was quiet. There was nobody outside except for some guy working on the engine of his car. Inside one of the houses a baby was crying. A sprinkler sputtered in circles in one of the yards.

I walked up the road toward the house. I hummed a little so my face wouldn't look as nervous as I felt.

When I walked by the man working on his car engine, he didn't even look up. I strolled along beside the hedge that surrounded the big brick house. I quit humming so I could listen. It was quiet in the yard. I glanced back to make sure no one was watching me, then poked my head over the gate to look into the yard.

Birds flew away from a bird feeder that hung from a hickory nut tree. The front door of the house was closed, and I noticed something I hadn't seen the other day—one of those little doggie doors, so the dog could go in and out of the house all by hisself. I figured that was a good sign. It probably meant that the people who lived there were gone a lot, but they still cared about their dog.

Then I remembered my rule about checking to see if the gate was locked. I reached over and lifted the latch. Nope. Not locked.

Suddenly a squirrel came scampering around the corner of the house and scrambled up the hickory nut tree. Not far behind it was the black-and-white dog. He dashed to the tree and peered up into the branches with his tail wagging about a million times a minute.

"Hey there," I called to him.

He sat in the leaves under the tree and cocked his head at me. His face was white with little black spots, like freckles, and black fur around one eye, like a patch. His ears were floppy, but when he looked at me, they perked up. But the best thing about him was that he looked like he was smiling at me. The sides of his mouth curled up and his pink tongue hung out.

"Hey there," I said again.

His doggie smile got bigger and his tail wagged harder, swishing leaves back and forth.

"Come here, fella." I reached over the gate and

snapped my fingers at him. He came trotting right over. I stooped down and stuck my fingers through the chain-link fence. He sniffed and then he licked me a couple of times.

"How you doing, little fella?" I said.

He cocked his head again and looked so cute.

I looked at the house. The front door was still closed and it seemed like nobody was home. I scratched the dog behind his ears, and he leaned his head against my hand with his eyes closed. He was wearing two collars. One was a dirty plastic flea collar. The other one was green with shiny rhinestones and a little silver tag shaped like a dog bone.

"What does this say?" I pulled the dog a little closer and squinted at the words engraved on the tag.

Willy, it said.

I turned it over. On the other side it said:

Carmella Whitmore
27 Whitmore Road
Darby, NC

Under that was a phone number.

"Willy," I whispered to the dog.

His floppy ears perked up, and he did that dog smile thing again.

"My name is Georgina," I said to Willy.

Just then that squirrel made its way down the trunk

of the hickory nut tree, and Willy dashed off to chase it again.

I stood up and looked around. Way at the end of the street, two kids were riding bikes. The man who had been working on his car was sitting in a lawn chair smoking a cigarette.

Uh-oh, I thought. *What if he saw me?*

I headed back up the street, trying to look like a normal person instead of a person who was thinking about stealing a dog. I kept my head down and concentrated on keeping my feet from running. I didn't look at the man when I passed him, but I caught a whiff of cigarette smoke.

When I got to the corner, I finally let my feet run like they'd been wanting to, all the way back to the car. When I got there, I unlocked the door and climbed in behind the steering wheel.

I put my hand on my racing heart and laid my head against the seat. I was starting to wonder if I really could steal a dog. I'd never stolen anything in my whole life. Luanne did one time. Slipped a pack of M&M's right into her coat pocket. But not me. How in the world was I going to steal that dog?

But then I looked around me at all the stuff inside our car. The Styrofoam cooler full of icy water and plastic containers of tuna salad. The trash bags stuffed with clothes and shoes. The milk crate on the floor with paper towels, shampoo, a flashlight, a can opener.

I looked into the backseat on Toby's side of the car. His blanket all smooshed up in a ball. His pillow. His Scooby-Doo pajamas.

And then there was my side, with all my special things jammed into a plastic bag instead of sitting out on my dresser like they used to. My horse statue. My swimming medals. That little stuffed bear that I got in the Smoky Mountains.

I hated every inch of that car. I put both hands on the steering wheel and pretended like I was driving. I drove and I drove and I drove, the whole time sending bad thoughts to my daddy for getting tired of it all and making us live in a car.

And as I drove along, out of Darby, out of North Carolina, on and on and on, as far as I could go, I felt better about what I had to do. I had to steal that little dog, Willy. No matter what.

5

I watched Luanne and Liza Thomas walking to the bus after school, their matching blond ponytails swinging from side to side. They carried their ballet slippers in their Darby Dance School tote bags.

Instead of getting on the bus and taking my usual seat beside Luanne, I had to wait for Toby so we could go to the Laundromat. I watched everybody get on the bus in their perfect clothes so they could go home to their perfect bedrooms. They'd put their school clothes away in real drawers, not trash bags. Then they'd go to soccer practice or ballet class, not to the Laundromat like me.

I blinked hard and stared down at my feet, just in case I looked as miserable as I felt. The toe of my sneaker was wearing out and I could see my blue sock starting to show through. When I heard someone running, I looked up to see Toby racing toward me, his hair flopping down in his eyes.

"Hurry up," I snapped. "I've been waiting for, like, an hour."

"I got on the bus but then I remembered I wasn't supposed to," he said.

Oh, great, I thought. I bet Luanne and Liza had themselves a good laugh about that. I bet Liza said, "How come Georgina and Toby aren't riding the bus?" Then what would Luanne say? *Please, please, Luanne.* I closed my eyes and tried to send my thoughts across the parking lot and into the school bus window where Luanne sat. *Please don't tell Liza we live in a car.*

Then I hurried up the sidewalk toward town. Toby trotted along behind me, whining for me to slow down, but I didn't. We headed on over to Montgomery Street where Mama had parked the car near the Laundromat. I unlocked the trunk and tossed my backpack inside. Then I stood on the bumper of the car so I could reach way in the back of the trunk. I pulled a corner of the carpet away and took out the envelope Mama kept hidden there. I thumbed through the money stuffed inside. It sure looked like a lot to me, but I guess it still wasn't enough to get us a place to live.

I took out five dollars and jammed the envelope back under the carpet. Then I gathered up the dirty laundry and locked the car.

"Let's go, Toby."

I stuffed all the clothes into one washing machine.

"If we don't use two machines," I said to Toby, "we'll have enough money to buy a snack."

On the way out, we checked all the coin return slots for money and found two quarters. Then we went on over to the grocery store and bought some saltine crackers and sliced cheese. We went around back to the alley and sat on the warm asphalt to eat.

"Listen, Toby," I said while I peeled the plastic off my cheese. "We need to find some kind of rope or something to tie to that dog's collar."

Toby nodded as he squished a piece of cheese into a little ball and popped it into his mouth.

"Where can we find rope?" I said.

He shrugged.

"Dern it, Toby," I said. "If you want to help me, you've got to come up with some ideas, too, you know. I can't think of everything."

"Okay," he said. "Why don't we buy some rope?"

I rolled my eyes. "We're trying to *save* our money, not spend it. We need to find some rope for free."

Toby looked around him at the piles of cardboard boxes beside the Dumpster. "Maybe there's rope back here somewhere."

I got up and peered into the Dumpster. Just more cardboard boxes.

"Naw," I said. "I think we're going to have to wait till trash pickup day. Then we can look through the stuff that people leave by the road, okay?"

"Okay." Toby squished another piece of cheese and then smashed it between two crackers.

"Let's go put the clothes in the dryer, then check out that dog again."

When we got to Whitmore Road, I motioned for Toby to be quiet.

"We don't want anybody to notice us," I whispered.

We made our way up the road toward the big brick house. When we got to the corner of the yard, I could hear someone out front. I tried to see through the hedge, but it was too thick. I squatted down beside the fence to listen.

"Get the ball, Willy," someone said. I was pretty sure it was the same woman we had seen there the other day.

I could hear Willy making happy little yip noises. Then the woman would laugh and say stuff to him. After a while, I heard the wooden front steps creak and the screen door slam.

I looked at Toby. "I think she went inside," I whispered. "Let's go see."

We tiptoed to the gate and I peeked into the yard. The woman was gone, but Willy was sitting on the front porch. When he saw me, he came bounding down the steps and over to the gate.

"Hey there, Willy," I whispered.

He pushed his nose through the gate and licked my hand.

"Isn't he cute?" I said to Toby.

"Yeah." Toby put his hand out and Willy licked him, too. "When are we gonna steal him?"

"Shhhh." I smacked Toby's knee. "Hush up, you idiot." I looked around us. The street was quiet and empty. I could hear a radio somewhere in the distance, but I didn't see anyone.

"We have to wait till everything is just right," I said. "That lady has to be gone." I nodded toward the house. "And we need some rope, remember?"

"After we get the rope and steal him, where are we going to hide him?" Toby said.

Dang! I hadn't even thought of that! I couldn't hardly believe how stupid I'd been. I'd made all those plans and hadn't even thought about where we were going to *hide* that dog!

I looked at Willy and then back at Toby. "I haven't figured that part out yet," I said, pretending like it was no big deal. "You got any ideas?"

Toby shook his head.

I frowned. "Then we'll have to think of something."

That night, I propped the flashlight up on the seat next to me and tried to do my math homework. Toby's snores drifted through the beach towel wall between us. I used to be good at math, but it seemed like now I wasn't. I gave up and took out my purple notebook. I opened to:

How to Steal a Dog
by
Georgina Hayes

I wrote *April* 7. Then, after *Step* 2, I wrote:

Step 3: Get ready to steal the dog.
1. Keep watching the dog to make sure he is the right one to steal.
2. If you need a leash, find some rope or something.
3. Figure out where you are going to hide the dog.

I chewed on the eraser of my pencil and stared out the window into the darkness. Number 3 was a big problem. I wished I could ask Luanne to help me. She always had good ideas about stuff. I looked down at my notebook again. I guessed I was just going to have to figure this out by myself, unless some miracle happened and Toby got an idea.

I closed the notebook and watched the moths fluttering around the streetlight outside the window. Maybe stealing a dog wasn't such a good idea after all. I propped my feet up on the seat in front of me and frowned at my bare toes. My Party Girl Pink nail polish was wearing off and I didn't have any more. I guess it got tossed out with all my other stuff.

"We can't take everything, Georgina," Mama had

hollered at me when Mr. Deeter kicked us out. "One bag," she had said in a mean voice. "That's it."

Just when I was starting to feel a good cry coming on, I heard Mama hurrying toward the car. I sat up and rolled down the window.

"Georgina," she whispered real excited-like. "Guess what?"

"What?"

"I found us a place!"

"Really?" I felt my heavy heart start to lift.

Mama put both hands against the car door and grinned down at me. Her hair was damp and frizzy from working her second job in the steamy back room of the Regal Dry Cleaners. She took her shoes off and climbed into the front seat.

"Yep! We're moving into a house!"

We had only ever lived in apartments before. *Never* in a house. I could already see my bedroom. White furniture with gold on the edges, like Luanne's. Maybe even pink carpet.

"When?" I said.

"Friday." Mama examined herself in the rear-view mirror.

"I look as beat as I feel, don't I?" she said.

"You look all right," I said, but I was lying. She did look beat. Dark circles under her eyes. Her skin all creased and greasy-looking.

I lay back against the seat and felt about a hundred pounds lighter than I had just minutes before. I'd known in my heart that stealing a dog was a bad thing to do, and now I didn't have to. I couldn't believe everything had turned out so good.

6

My stomach was flopping around like crazy as we made our way through the neighborhoods of Darby. I couldn't hardly wait to see which house would be ours.

But when Mama turned onto a dirt and gravel road, I started to get a bad feeling. The car squeaked and bounced up the narrow, winding road, deeper and deeper into the woods. When we passed a faded, hand-written sign nailed to a tree, my bad feeling got worse. KEEP OUT. PRIVATE PROPERTY.

"Are you sure this is right?" I said to Mama.

She clutched the steering wheel and sat up straight and tense. "Yes, Georgina," she said. "I know what I'm doing, okay?"

Then, just as I thought my bad feeling couldn't get any worse, we rounded a curve and I saw a house just ahead of us. A ramshackle old house with boarded-up windows and the front door hanging all cockeyed on its rusty hinges.

Mama stopped the car and we all three stared in silence at the wreck of a house. The tar paper roof was caved in and covered with rotting leaves and pine needles. Prickly-looking bushes grew thick and dense across the front, while kudzu vines snaked their way up the chimney and across the roof.

"Well," Mama said, "It ain't Shangri-la, but it's better than nothing."

I couldn't believe my ears.

"*That's* the house we're gonna live in?" I said.

"It's just temporary." Mama turned the engine off and started throwing stuff into a cardboard box on the seat beside her. "Beverly Jenkins over at the Handy Pantry knows the owner, and she said he won't care if we stay here for a while."

Toby started crying. "I don't want to," he whined.

"Hush up, Toby," Mama said. She got out and tried to push through the bushes that grew across the front of the house. "Come on, y'all," she said. "Let's check it out."

I crossed my arms and slumped down in the seat. This just beat all. First I had to go and get a daddy who acted mean all the time and then just up and left us. Now I had a mama who had gone plumb crazy.

"Come on, Georgina," Mama called. "It's not that bad."

She had managed to get to the front door and had pushed it open to peer inside.

"Really, y'all," she said. "We can clean it up and make it nice."

Toby was sniffling, and I knew he was waiting on me to make the first move.

"I bet there's snakes in there," I called out through the car window.

Mama had disappeared inside, but her voice came drifting out to us. "There's no snakes. There's even some furniture. Come on."

I looked at Toby and he looked at me.

"You think there's really snakes in there?" he said.

"Snakes and worse," I said. "Probably rats and spiders and dead stuff."

Toby started wailing. Mama came out and made her way back to the car, pushing the bushes aside to make a path. "Come on," she said, opening the door and gathering up the box and trash bags and stuff.

"No," I said. "I'm staying here."

"No," Toby said. "I'm staying here."

Mama slammed the box down and yanked the back door open.

"Listen here," she hollered. "I'm doing the best I can. At least we'll have a roof over our heads and some room to spread out. It won't be for long."

"How long?" I said.

She sighed. "Not long," she said. "I almost have enough for rent, but most places want a deposit, too.

You two just don't get it." Her voice started getting louder until she was hollering again. "You think all I got to do is snap my fingers and *bingo!*" She pounded on top of the car. "*There's* the rent and *there's* the deposit and *there's* the gas for the car," she yelled. "And *snap*, there's electricity and water and phone. Not to mention food and clothes and doctors and STUFF." She kicked the car when she yelled the word "stuff."

Toby and I jumped.

"Now get out of the dern car and come inside," she said. Then she picked up the box and started back through the bushes toward the house.

I gathered up my pillow and our beach towel wall. "Come on, Toby," I said. "Let's go."

The house smelled damp and moldy. The floor was littered with leaves and acorns. In the front room, a lumpy couch stood underneath the plywood-covered window. Mice or rats or something had chewed through the fabric to the foam stuffing beneath. Stacks of yellowing newspapers were piled in one corner. Two empty cans of pork and beans sat on a rusty wood stove.

I followed Mama into the kitchen. The cracked linoleum floor was sticky and made squeaky noises as we walked across it. I wrinkled my nose and peered into the sink. Twigs and dirt that had fallen through a hole in the ceiling floated in a puddle of dark brown water. I turned the faucet, but no water came out. Not even one little drop. In one corner of the kitchen, a wobbly table was covered with empty soda cans and beer bottles. Cigarette butts were scattered on the floor beneath it.

"Our nasty ole car is better than this place," I said, but Mama acted like she didn't hear me. She set the box on the table and pushed her hair out of her face.

"Y'all bring the rest of our stuff in and let's start cleaning this place up," she said.

That night, I lay on the floor on top of piled-up clothes, covered with my beach towel, and stared at the mildewed ceiling.

In one corner, rain had leaked in and left a dark spot.

I narrowed my eyes, and that dark spot looked just like Willy. His ears and his eyes and even his whiskers. That morning, I had pushed him right out of my mind and now here he was back again, all because of this awful old house.

I could hear Mama tossing and turning on the other side of the room. Toby was curled up next to me. Every now and then his leg jerked. I bet he was dreaming about spiders and snakes.

I wanted more than anything to go to sleep so I wouldn't have to think about stuff, but I couldn't. I just lay there thinking about how everything had gotten so messed up and all. Then I remembered an Aesop's fable that Mr. White had read us in school. The one about the hares and the frogs. I could still hear him reading the moral at the end. "There is always someone worse off than yourself."

Ha! I thought. Ole Mr. Aesop must have been stupid 'cause he was just flat-out wrong. There was nobody, nowhere, worse off than me.

7

I studied myself in the mirror of the bathroom at McDonald's. My hair hung in greasy clumps on my forehead. Creases from the crumpled-up clothes I had slept on were still etched in the side of my face. I rubbed my hands together under the water and ran my wet fingers through my hair. Then I used paper towels to scrub my face and arms. The rough brown paper left my skin red and scratched.

We'd spent the weekend in that old house and I was beginning to think I'd rather sleep in the car again. Mama had got some stuff at a yard sale to try to make things better. A plastic raft for us to take turns sleeping on. A radio that ran on batteries. An alarm clock. Stuff like that. She even got a great big artificial plant with red and purple flowers. She had wiped the dust off the leaves with her shirttail and set it up on top of the wood stove. I guess she thought that plant would make me glad to be there, but it didn't. If things didn't change soon, I was going to have to go back to my dog-stealing plans. That's all there was to it.

The bathroom door opened and Mama stuck her head inside.

"We got to go, Georgina," she said. "I can't be late for work again."

I followed her out to the car. I couldn't help but notice how her blue jeans hung all baggy, dragging on the asphalt parking lot as she walked. I guess she was getting skinnier.

She had on her green Handy Pantry T-shirt. Her long fingers clutched a cup of coffee that sent trails of steam into the early morning air.

"I'll drop y'all off at the corner," she said, climbing into the car. "Then go on up yonder to the bus stop, okay?"

"Okay." I got into the backseat beside Toby and propped my feet on top of my bag of stuff. Mama had told us not to leave our things in that nasty ole house, "just in case." When I'd asked "Just in case what?" she had flapped her hand at me and told me to stop asking so many questions.

"After school," she said, "you and Toby wait in the car while I work at the cleaners, then we'll go on back to the house after that, okay?"

I stuffed my notebook into my backpack. Today was the day we were supposed to bring in our science projects. I didn't have mine, but I didn't even care. I'd tell Mr. White my project got lost or stolen or something.

"Okay, Georgina?" Mama said, craning her neck to look at me in the rearview mirror.

"I guess." I stared out the window.

"What's the matter?"

I shrugged. "Nothing."

"Come on and tell me, Georgina," she said. "What's the matter?"

I felt a wave of mad sweep over me. "*Everything!*" I hollered. "Okay? *Everything's* the matter."

I kept my head turned toward the window, but I could feel her eyes on me.

"Give me a break, okay?" she yelled into the mirror. "You're just making this harder on everybody, Miss Glum and Angry. What would you like me to do, rob a bank?"

Toby giggled and I shot him a look that wiped the grin right off his face.

"Maybe you could act like a *mother*," I said.

Mama slammed on the brakes and whipped around to glare at me.

"Just what is *that* supposed to mean?" she said.

"Mothers are supposed to take care of their kids," I said. "Not let them sleep in creepy old houses and wash up in the bathroom at McDonald's."

Mama pressed her lips together and I could tell she was thinking hard about what to say. But then she just sighed and turned back around.

We rode in silence the rest of the way. When we got to the corner near the bus stop, I got out and slammed the door. Hard.

"Look after Toby, okay, Georgina," Mama called after me.

"Yeah," I said. "Whatever."

"Was he mad?" Luanne asked me as we headed toward the bus.

"Naw."

"What did he say?"

"Nothing."

"Nothing?"

"Well, I mean, nothing much." I didn't look at Luanne 'cause I knew she would know I was lying. Mr. White had said plenty. He'd said how he couldn't understand my bad attitude lately. And he was so disappointed in my lack of effort recently. And then he had to go and ask me if everything was all right at home.

I had kept my eyes on the Styrofoam planets dangling from a coat hanger behind him. Somebody's stupid science project.

"Yessir," I said. "Everything's fine."

Then he had given me another envelope with *Mr. and Mrs. Hayes* written on it. Would I be sure and have my parents call him, he had said.

And if he didn't hear from them, he was going to have to talk to the principal about the problem. Did I understand, he had said.

"Yessir," I told him. What I didn't tell him was that my daddy was long gone and my mama couldn't even get us a place to live and my things got thrown out with the garbage. I didn't tell him that my best friend didn't even like me anymore and now she had a new friend. All I said to him was "Yessir."

I stuffed the envelope way down inside my backpack and left quick as I could.

On the bus, Luanne and I took our regular seats, and then Liza Thomas got on and stopped beside us.

"Are you going to Girl Scouts today?" she asked Luanne. She had on a red T-shirt with sparkly gold glitter spelling out *Cool Chick*.

"Yeah, are you?" Luanne said.

"Yeah." Liza flicked her ponytail behind her shoulder. "I'll see you there, okay?"

"Okay."

I could feel my jealousy churning around inside. Girl Scouts. I could just see Luanne and Liza there, side by side, working on their outdoor cooking badge or maybe planning a visit to the nursing home. I had to drop out of Girl Scouts so I could take care of Toby after school. Besides, I couldn't pay the dues or go on the trip to Six Flags or anything.

When we got off the bus, Liza waved at us out the window. Luanne waved back, but I didn't. Toby trotted along behind us.

"Wanna come over to my house before Girl Scouts?" Luanne said.

I wanted to say yes more than anything. I wanted to go over to the Godfreys' and lie on Luanne's soft pink carpet, eating graham crackers and working on one of my Girl Scout badges.

"I can't," I said. And that was all.

Me and Toby went on down the hill to where Mama was waiting for us in the car. I hated looking at that beat-up old car with bags of stuff all piled up on the seats. Black smoke puffed out of the tailpipe and the engine made a rattly sound.

"Hey, y'all," Mama called through the open window. "Look what I got." She waved a giant bag of M&M's at us.

"Hot dang!" Toby hollered, racing to the car.

I yanked the door open, tossed my backpack inside, and climbed in. Toby was already ripping the candy bag open.

"I don't want any," I said. Then I took my social studies book out of my backpack and pretended to read Chapter 21 like I was supposed to.

Mama turned around in the front seat. "Georgina," she said. "Please stop making this worse than it already is."

"I'm not."

"Yes you are." She got up on her knees and leaned over the seat to put her face down close to mine. "It won't be much longer now, I promise," she said.

"How much longer?"

Mama sighed. "A few more days maybe," she said.

A few more days? She might as well have said "forever."

I felt the tears running down my face and then Mama's warm hand on my cheek.

"I'm sorry, sweetheart," she said. "I swear, every night I pray for a miracle but I reckon nobody's listening."

"What kind of miracle?" I said. My voice sounded small and pitiful.

"I don't know," she said. "Anything. Money, mostly."

I nodded.

Okay, that does it, I said to myself. I was going to have to steal that dog, after all. I had to. It was the only way we were ever going to get ourselves out of this mess and live like normal people again.

So when Mama parked the car and kissed us good-bye, I pulled out my purple notebook and read through all my dog-stealing notes. I put a little checkmark beside the things I had already done. When I got to the part about finding a place to hide the dog, I thumped my pencil against my knee and thought real hard. Where in the world could I hide a dog? In the woods somewhere, maybe? Or over behind the Elks Lodge? Maybe in that old chicken coop out there by Hiram Foley's place?

I closed my notebook and stared out the window at the folks sitting in front of the Dairy Queen across the street.

Stealing a dog had seemed so easy when I'd first thought of it. Now it seemed like the hardest thing I'd ever done.

"Georgina?"

Toby's voice interrupted my thoughts.

"What?"

"Are we still gonna steal that dog?" he said.

"Yes," I said. "We are."

"When?"

"Soon." I pushed my notebook down under the clothes in my trash bag.

That night it was my turn to sleep on the plastic raft. Strips of moonlight poured through the cracks in the plywood that covered the windows, and danced across the dusty wooden floor. I tried to make myself stop thinking so I could go to sleep, but my mind just wouldn't turn off. I went through my plan over and over, imagining myself with that little dog, Willy. Picturing myself running with him in my arms. Seeing myself hiding him someplace. But where?

I threw the beach towel off of me and tiptoed over to

the corner of the room where my stuff was. I took out my notebook and sat down in a beam of moonlight so I could see. I turned to *Step 3* of *How to Steal a Dog*. I wrote *April 12*. Then, under the part that said: *3. Figure out where you are going to hide the dog*, I wrote:

a. The place where you hide the dog has to be close enough so you can go visit him.

b. The place has to be somewhere that nobody goes to or else they will see the dog and maybe turn him loose or call the dog pound or something.

c. Try to find a place that is a nice place for a dog to be.

d. Try to find a place that has a roof because what if it rains?

I tried to think of some more stuff, but I guess I was too tired. My mind was finally starting to slow down and stop thinking. So I wrote: *Now you are almost ready to steal a dog*, and put my notebook away.

I tiptoed back over to my raft bed. I pulled the beach towel up under my chin, closed my eyes, and slept a deep, dreamless sleep like I used to when I had a bed.

But I bet if I'd known what was going to happen the next day, I never would have slept that good.

8

I stared down at my desk, and in my head I begged Mr. White not to call on me.

"Georgina?" he said. "How about reading us your report on volcanoes?"

I looked at the paper in my hand. I had made my writing real big so I could fill up a whole page like we were supposed to. Everybody else had used their computers or gone to the library, but not me. All I could do was sit in that nasty house making stuff up.

With my face burning, I read my report about how volcanoes are like mountains with a hole in the middle and then fire comes out and hot lava runs down the side. My whole report lasted about two seconds and then it was over and everybody laughed. I was sure I could hear Luanne and Liza laughing louder than anybody else.

Mr. White said, "Shhhh," and put his hand on my shoulder.

"Thank you, Georgina," he said, and my heart swelled up with love for him. My report was nothing but great big made-up words, but he was still being nice to me. He wasn't going to holler at me like he had hollered at Luke Ketchum.

I hadn't been doing too good in school lately, but I still looked forward to being there. At least at school, I knew how my day was going to go. I knew we'd say the Pledge of Allegiance and then we'd raise our hands if we wanted grilled cheese instead of chicken fingers for lunch. Then we'd look up there on the chalkboard and our whole day would be written out. Math and then reading. A spelling test and then gym. No surprises.

Not like after school, when I never knew what was going to happen next. It seemed like something new was always coming my way, and most times it wasn't good. Like that very day of my volcano report, when me and Toby got back to the car and Mama was sitting there all red-faced and crying.

Toby lunged right through the open window and hugged her so hard I thought she was gonna choke. She peeled his arms from around her neck and said, "Y'all get in the car."

I got in my usual spot in the back, but Toby jumped in the front, pushing all the boxes and bags and things aside. He kept on saying, "What's the matter, Mama?" but she wouldn't answer.

Nobody said anything as we sped along the streets of Darby. Mama gripped the steering wheel with both hands, her knuckles white and her elbows locked stiff. When we stopped at a red light, she put her head down on the steering wheel. The light turned green and a big truck behind us honked but Mama didn't even look up.

"Mama?" I said.

Nothing. The truck horn honked again and somebody yelled.

"Mama?" I said again.

The truck roared around us and the man driving it hollered and shook his fist at us.

I had a feeling something bad was about to happen.

"The light's green," I said.

Mama lifted her head up off the steering wheel and stared out at the road. Another horn honked behind us.

"I got fired at the cleaners," she said. "Can you believe that?"

"How come?" I said.

Mama breathed out a big whoosh. "Who knows," she said, " 'Cause I was late once or twice, I reckon. Or 'cause I don't use that pressing machine fast enough. Or maybe just 'cause I'm alive."

She didn't even turn her head when another car whipped around us, honking like crazy.

"Maybe you better get out of the road," I said.

"Maybe I better get out of the whole dern world," she said, and sounded so mean. She swiped at tears and wiped her nose with her hand. "Maybe I better just disappear off the face of the earth. Poof! Like that." She snapped her fingers. "Wouldn't that be nice?"

I felt words bubbling up inside me till they came busting out.

"Yeah!" I hollered. "That *would* be nice."

I kicked the back of the seat and made Mama's head jerk but she kept staring straight ahead.

"Why *don't* you disappear, and then me and Toby can do what we want to. Right, Toby?" I poked the back of Toby's head, but he just rocked back and forth, sniffling.

Another car horn honked, and Mama sat up straight like she had just woke up. She brushed the hair out of her eyes and started driving again.

Nobody said anything as we turned down the dirt and gravel road that led to the house. The car squeaked and bounced and rattled. When we stopped, Mama turned off the engine and the car gave one last little shudder.

We gathered our things and made our way through the prickly bushes to the front porch. And then we all three stopped dead in our tracks and stared at that old house. Boards had been nailed in a giant X over the front door. Someone had written on the boards in great big letters, "This is private property! Keep out!" They had added about a million exclamation points, so it looked like this:

THIS IS PRIVATE PROPERTY! KEEP OUT!!!!!!!!!!!!!!

Mama dropped her stuff right off the porch and into the bushes. Blankets and pillows and everything. Then she sat down on the rickety steps and hollered out a bunch of cuss words that echoed through the woods.

Toby got all blubbery, but I just stood there looking at that boarded-up door. I was surprised how bad I felt, seeing as how I hated that house. But I guess it had been better than the car, after all.

I watched the back of Mama's head and I could almost see her sadness swirling around her.

"It's a good thing you made us take our stuff out of there every day," I said.

She just stared out at the woods. Toby was whimpering and pulling the blankets up out of the bushes.

"That would have been awful if our stuff was locked up in there," I said.

Mama kept staring out into the woods.

"I guess Beverly Jenkins was wrong about this house," I said. "I guess the owner doesn't want us here, after all."

Mama turned her head slowly and looked at me and her face didn't show anything. Not mad. Not sad. Not anything. Then she stood up and gathered the rest of the blankets and stuff.

"Come on, y'all," she said.

Me and Toby followed her out to the car and climbed in.

As we made our way back up the gravel road toward

the highway, I hummed a little bit, trying to clear the heavy air in the car.

"Georgina, *please*," Mama said. So I hushed up.

I stared out at the world passing by my window and I made up my mind. I was definitely gonna steal that dog.

9

That night, I dreamed Toby was a dog. He sat on the backseat beside me with his head stuck out the window, his ears flapping in the wind. We drove and drove and drove and then we pulled into a long, winding road that led to a castle. Mama stopped the car in front of the giant front door of the castle and said, "Here's our new house!"

Toby the dog started crying and saying how he wanted to go back home where he belonged.

And then I woke up. I peered down at Toby, curled up on the floor of the car sucking his thumb. It was so hot the windows were all steamed up. I rolled my window partway down. Then I leaned back and stared out at the lit-up sign of the Brushy Creek Lutheran Church.

I had gone to that church one time when I was little. With my friend Racene Wickham. We had made May baskets, weaving strips of pink and yellow construction paper, in and out, in and out. I had glued a pink pipe cleaner handle on mine and filled it with clover flowers for Mama.

I remember how on the way home, I'd been all squished in the backseat beside Racene's brothers and I'd clutched that May basket in my lap. I couldn't wait to give it to Mama, even though the clover flowers had wilted and were lying all droopy in the bottom of the basket. But when I got home, Mama and Daddy were yelling at each other and wouldn't even look at me when I tried to show them my May basket.

Racene had moved away to Florida, and now here I was, back here at that very same church, sleeping in my car.

When the sun came up, we headed over to the Pancake House to wash up and get some toast. The bread we had in the milk crate in the trunk of the car had turned green with mold, and Mama had tossed it out the window, right into the church parking lot.

"I want pancakes," Toby said, frowning down at his toast.

Mama sipped her coffee, squinting through the steam, and said, "No."

"Why not?" Toby whined.

Mama slammed the cup down, sloshing coffee onto the table. "Because you can't have everything you want," she said.

I ate my toast and watched Mama scoop all the little plastic tubs of jelly into her purse.

"Y'all go over to the Y after school and wait till I get there, okay?" she said.

"The Y?"

"Yes, Georgina, the Y."

The Darby YMCA was nothing but a room in the basement of the Town Hall. Some kids went there after school to play games and stuff while their parents were at work.

"We can't go *there*," I said.

Mama sighed. "Just do like I say, Georgina."

"But you have to sign up and stuff," I said. "You can't just *go* there. And I bet you have to pay."

But Mama wouldn't even answer me. She counted out some coins, slapped them on the table, and headed out to the car, leaving me and Toby to scramble after her.

That day in school, all I could think about was how I was going to steal that little dog, Willy. While Mr. White read stuff about the Revolutionary War, I pulled my purple notebook out of my backpack and flipped to the *How to Steal a Dog* page. I read through what I had so far. Everything seemed pretty good except for that problem about where to keep the dog after you steal him.

I thought and thought about it, and then, just like a lightbulb going on, I got an idea. I could keep Willy at that boarded-up old house! There was a tiny little porch around back off the kitchen. It was kind of rotten and all, but a dog wouldn't care about that. And that house wasn't too far from Whitmore Road. I could walk that far, no problem. At last, I thought, things were finally starting to look better.

At lunch, I asked Luanne if me and Toby could go to her house after school. I didn't tell her we were supposed to go to the Y.

"Um, I don't think so," Luanne said.

"How come?"

Luanne fiddled with the buttons on her shirt. "I got some stuff to do," she said.

"Like what?"

She shrugged. "Just some stuff with Mama."

I twirled my spaghetti around and around on my fork and listened to the girls at our table going on and on about some movie they'd all seen. Then Luanne piped in and said how she had just loved that movie, too. I kept on twirling my spaghetti and feeling more and more like I didn't want to be there at that lunch table. I wanted to float right up through the ceiling and out into the blue sky. I didn't belong there with those girls. I hadn't seen that movie. I couldn't buy those bracelets they all wore. They had been over at the mall while I'd been washing my underwear in the bathroom sink at Walgreens.

So I just sat there twirling and thinking about Willy.

After school, me and Toby walked over to the Town Hall.

"I'm not going down there," I told him, nodding toward the basement window. "You can if you want to, but I'm not." The sound of kids playing and balls bouncing drifted out of the open window.

Toby shook his head. "Then I'm not going neither," he said.

I tossed my backpack on a nearby bench. "We've got to find some string or something," I said to Toby.

"What for?"

"For Willy. Remember?"

"Oh."

So we walked up and down the street, looking in gutters and Dumpsters and trash cans. I was just about to give up when Toby hollered, "Here's some, Georgina!"

I ran over to the curb where Toby was holding a stack of newspapers tied with heavy string.

"Yes!" I pumped my fist and high-fived Toby. "Good job!" Toby looked just pleased as punch. I untied the string and stuffed it into my pocket. "Let's go back and wait for Mama," I said.

It was nearly dark by the time we saw our car come sputtering up the street toward the Town Hall, leaving a trail of black smoke behind it.

"Sorry, y'all," Mama said when we climbed in the backseat.

"We're starving," Toby said.

"I know, sweetheart," Mama said. "I brought y'all some chicken."

Toby dug through the bag in the front seat and pulled out a piece of greasy fried chicken.

"I got a job," Mama said.

I took a piece of chicken and pulled the soggy skin off. "Where?" I said, dropping the chicken skin back into the bag.

"The coffee shop over by the hardware store." She glanced at herself in the rearview mirror. I wondered if she saw the same tired and worried face that I did.

"Well, that's good," I said.

She took a swig out of a soda can. "I guess so," she said, then pulled the car to the side of the road and stopped.

"What's the matter?" I said.

She shook her head. "I'm just so dern tired of all this," she said.

My stomach clumped up in a knot, and I wished I hadn't eaten that chicken. Why was Mama acting so sad? I needed her to act like everything was okay.

Nobody said anything after that. We just sat there in that car that was our home. Crammed in with all of our stuff. The smell of the greasy fried chicken hovered in the still air around us.

Mama broke the silence when she slapped her hands on the steering wheel and said, "Anyway, so now I'll be at work when y'all get out of school. So come on over to the coffee shop and wait in the car, okay?"

I ran my dog-stealing plans around inside my head. This would be perfect. The coffee shop wasn't far from Whitmore Road. I could grab Willy, hide him on the porch of the old house, and then get on back to the car, no problem. Mama wouldn't even know if me and Toby were there or not.

That night, I fingered the string in my pocket and watched Mama helping Toby with his homework. They huddled together in the front seat with the flashlight propped up on the dashboard. Shadows danced around on the ceiling as they worked.

I pulled out my notebook and turned to *How to Steal a Dog*. I wrote *April 14*, then, beside that:

Step 4: Use this list to make sure you are ready to steal a dog.
1. Are you sure you have found the right dog?
Yes ___ No ___
2. Can you open the gate?
Yes ___ No ___
3. Do you have some rope or string?
Yes ___ No ___

4. Do you have a good place to keep the dog?
Yes ___ No ___

I read through each one and put a checkmark beside *Yes* every time.

After the list, I wrote: *If you can check "yes" for every one, then you are ready to steal a dog.*

I thumped the pencil eraser against my teeth, then I added:

P.S. Remember that you have to wait until nobody is home at the house where the dog lives.
P.P.S. Don't forget to take your string, rope, or leash.

I closed my notebook and pushed it back down inside my trash bag. And when my guilty conscience started hollering at me, telling me I was doing the wrong thing, I pushed that down, too.

There was no doubt about it. I really, really was going to steal a dog.

10

Shhhh." I put my finger to my lips and motioned for Toby to stay behind me. We tiptoed along the hedge in front of the big brick house. When we got to the gate, I scanned the street, then whispered to Toby.

"You be the lookout. If anybody comes outside or a car comes or *anything*, you whistle like I showed you this morning, okay?"

Toby nodded.

I peered over the gate. The front door of the house was closed. I glanced toward the driveway. No car. The yard was empty and quiet.

"Here, Willy," I called out real soft. Nothing. Maybe he was inside. I wondered if I should go on up to the porch. Probably not. If somebody *was* home, they were liable to see me.

"Maybe you should whistle," Toby whispered.

"Okay." I whistled one time and waited. Sure enough, Willy stuck his head out of that little doggie door. When he saw me, he dashed out the door and up to the gate.

"Hey, Willy," I whispered, sticking my hand through the gate to pet him.

He stood on his hind legs and put his front paws on the gate. His tail wagged so hard his whole body wiggled. He licked my hand like it was a T-bone steak.

"You wanna come with us?" I said.

He cocked his head and peered up at me. And then, I swear, he nodded his head. If he could've talked, I was sure he would've said, "Heck, yeah, I wanna come with you."

So, quick as I could, I lifted the latch on the gate and opened it just enough to reach my arm in. My heart was pounding so hard all I could hear was the thump, thump, thump in my ears. I knew I had to keep myself moving or else I was liable to start thinking. And if I started thinking, I was liable to think I shouldn't be doing this. So I turned my mind to "off" and grabbed Willy's collar. I pulled him through the gate and out onto the sidewalk. He kept wagging his tail and looking at me with his shiny black eyes. I took the string out of my pocket and tied it to his flea collar.

"Okay, let's go," I said to Toby, and took off running.

I ran down Whitmore Road, around the corner, and into the woods. Willy ran along beside me. Every now and then he leaped up on me or nipped at my heels like this was the most fun game he'd ever played. Once in a while he'd let out a little yip.

When we were far enough into the woods that I was

sure no one could see us from the road, I stopped to catch my breath. I put my hand on my pounding heart and leaned against a tree. Toby ran up and stopped beside me.

"We did it!" he hollered.

"Shhhh." I clamped my hand over his mouth. "Somebody might hear us. You got to be really quiet."

Willy sat in front of us with his tongue hanging out, panting. His tail wagged on the ground. Swish, swish, swish.

I knelt down and ran my hand along his back. He closed his eyes and leaned against me.

"It's okay, fella," I said. "Don't be scared. Me and Toby are nice."

He scratched behind his ear with his hind leg, making the tag on his collar jingle.

"What do we do now?" Toby said.

"We take him over to that house and tie him up on the porch."

"What if he don't like it there?"

"He's just gonna be there for a little while," I said. "As soon as his owner puts up the reward sign, we'll take him back home."

"Oh." Toby knelt and rubbed the top of Willy's head. "What if his owner don't put up a reward sign?"

I flapped my hand at Toby. "Trust me. That lady is gonna want him back more than anything. She's probably making a reward sign right now."

I made my voice sound calm and sure, but a funny little feeling was tapping at my insides. A feeling like maybe I had done a real bad thing. I took a deep breath, trying to swallow that feeling down and keep it from growing.

I unbuckled Willy's green collar and tossed it into the bushes. Tap, tap. There was that feeling again. Tapping at my insides like it was trying to tell me something.

"What'd you do that for?" Toby said.

I rolled my eyes. "Think about it, Toby."

Toby's eyebrows squeezed together and he bit his lip. " 'Cause he don't need it anymore?" he said.

I sighed. "No, *dum*-bo. Because we can't take him back to his owner with his collar on or else she'd wonder how come we didn't call her. Her phone number's right there on the tag."

"Oh." Toby nodded, but he still looked confused. I swear sometimes he is dumber than dirt.

"Come on." I motioned for Toby to follow me. We made our way through the woods behind the houses on Whitmore Road. I could hear the cars on the highway up ahead, so I was pretty sure we were going in the right direction.

Willy trotted along beside me happy as anything. Every now and then, he stopped to sniff the ground or root through the rotting leaves. Once, he stopped to dig, sending dirt and leaves and twigs flying out behind him and making me and Toby laugh. He sure was a funny dog.

When we got to the highway, I stooped down behind the bushes along the edge.

I handed the string leash to Toby. "Here," I said. "Hold this while I see if any cars are coming."

I checked in both directions. No cars. I went back to where Toby sat with his arm around Willy.

"Okay, now listen," I said. "We got to run across the highway, then through that vacant lot over there. I'm pretty sure we can cut through those woods to get to that old house."

He nodded.

I took the string from him and dashed across the highway with Willy leaping along beside me. We kept running until we made it to the edge of the gravel road leading to the old house. The whole time, Willy pranced and yipped and jumped up on me. Once in a while, he grabbed the string in his mouth and gave it a tug.

When we got to the house, Willy perked his ears up and watched me.

"We're here, fella," I said, scratching the top of his head.

He looked at that run-down, boarded-up house and then back at me. I had a feeling I knew what he was thinking.

"It's okay, Willy," I said. "You won't be here long. I promise."

He cocked his head in that cute way of his. I don't know how he did it, but that little dog could make you love him just by looking at him. I sat down in the dusty road and put my arm around him. He crawled right into my lap and licked my face. His licks weren't all slobbery like most dogs'.

"It's spooky here," Toby said in that whiny voice of his. I knew if I didn't do something fast, he was liable to turn into his baby self and start crying or something.

"You hold Willy and I'll make a path to the back porch," I said.

I pushed through the sticker bushes and vines, mashing them down and breaking off branches till there was a clear path to the back of the house. It was dark and damp back there. You couldn't even see the sky through the overgrown trees.

The tiny porch leaned slightly, like any minute it was going to fall right off the back of the house. The steps leading up to it were loose and rotten. One of them was broken all the way through. The screen door dangled by one hinge.

"Come on," I called to Toby.

He and Willy came around the corner of the house and stopped.

"No way, Georgina," Toby said. "We can't put Willy in there."

"Listen, Toby," I said. "This is the best place. No-body'll see him. And he won't get wet if it rains. And besides, he won't be here long." I watched Toby's face, but he didn't look convinced. "And we'll come and stay with him after school and all," I added.

Toby swiped at the tears that had started. "You're mean," he said.

Dern. Why'd he have to go and say that? I sure didn't want to hear it—'cause that was exactly how I was feeling. Mean.

"Toby, listen." I put both hands on his shoulders and looked him square in the eye. "Aren't you tired of living in the car?"

He hung his head and nodded a tiny little bit.

"Don't you want to have a *real* place to live? With walls and beds and a bathroom and all?"

He nodded again.

"Then we need to help Mama get some money," I said. "And this is the only thing I can think of. Can you think of another way?"

I bent down and tried to look him in the eye again, but his head was hanging too low. All I could see was his long, dirty hair all tangled up and ratty-looking.

"Then we got to do this," I said. "We'll take good care of Willy, and we'll take him right back home just as soon as we can, and then we'll get the reward money and everything will be good." I jiggled Toby's shoulders. "Okay?" I added.

I knew Toby didn't believe me 'cause I wasn't sure I believed myself. That old tapping feeling was getting bigger, and in my head I was thinking maybe I was messing up. And I was starting to think how I wished I could go back in time to the hour before or the day before or the week before. But I knew I couldn't do that. I was there behind that awful old house with that cute little dog looking at me, and I knew it was up to me to make everything turn out good like I had planned.

I took the string leash from Toby and led Willy up the creaky steps to the porch.

"This isn't so bad," I called out to Toby.

The top half of the porch had been screened in once, but now what was left of the rusty old screen hung in tatters. Leaves and pine needles had blown in and covered the floor, settling in the corners in damp, moldy piles.

I pushed some of the wet leaves aside, trying to make a clean spot. Then I knelt down and took Willy's head in both my hands.

"Don't be scared, okay?" I said. "We'll be back real soon and everything will be fine." Then I rubbed my nose back and forth against his. An Eskimo kiss.

Willy rested his chin in my hands and gazed up at me like he believed every word I said.

"What if he gets hungry?" Toby called from the bottom of the steps.

Hungry? I hadn't even thought about that! I couldn't believe Toby was thinking up something else I had left out of my *How to Steal a Dog* notes.

"I *said*, what if he gets hungry?" Toby called out.

"I've got that all worked out," I lied. My mind raced, trying to think of how I was going to feed Willy. And what if I couldn't get back here every day? How long could a dog go without food?

"And water," Toby said. "Dogs need water, you know. He might die if he don't have water."

"Shut up, Toby." That's all I could think of to say, and it did the trick. He shut up. But it didn't help me feel any better.

I tied the string to the doorknob and said goodbye to Willy. Then I led the way back through the weeds and briar bushes toward the road.

I was glad Toby was quiet as we walked, 'cause I had a lot of thinking to do. About food and water for Willy. About what I'd done. About what to do next. But it was hard to get my thoughts all straightened out with my insides kicking up like they were. That tapping feeling was turning into full-out banging.

11

Hey, y'all," Mama called as she made her way across the parking lot toward the car. "Look what I got."

She stuck a Styrofoam box through the window. "Check this out," she said.

I opened the box. Scrambled eggs and pancakes. They sure did smell good.

"And that's not all," she said, tossing a paper bag onto the backseat.

Toby snatched the bag up and peered inside, then let out a whoop. "Doughnuts!" he hollered. He grabbed a powdery white doughnut and started eating it so fast he choked, coughing out a spray of powder and crumbs.

"Eeeyew," I said, wiping off my jeans.

Mama slid behind the steering wheel and examined herself in the mirror. "This job is gonna be great," she said, licking a finger and smoothing an eyebrow. "The tips are really good and I get to bring home all kinds of food."

Food? Talk about good luck! Now we wouldn't have to worry about feeding Willy. I poked Toby and gave him a thumbs-up. His eyebrows shot up and he mouthed "What?" at me.

I flapped my hand at him to signal *never mind*, but he wouldn't be quiet. He kept whispering, "What?"

I shook my head and pulled an invisible zipper across my lips, which meant "Hush up, I can't tell you in front of Mama," but he was too dumb to figure that out.

"What?" he said a little louder.

"What'd you say?" Mama said.

I pressed my foot on top of Toby's and smiled at Mama in the rearview mirror. "Nothing," I said.

I settled back and ate some pancakes, which sure did taste good even though they were all soggy with syrup. When I finished, I took out my notebook and wrote: *Save some doughnuts for Willy.* I pushed the notebook across the seat and poked Toby.

He squinted down at my note. Then he grinned and said, "Ohhhhh, okay."

"What?" Mama said.

I jabbed my heel into Toby's foot and he hollered, "Owwww!"

Mama whirled around and snapped, "What're y'all doing?"

I slapped my hand over the note and smiled at her. "Nothing."

"Well, don't y'all start that bickering back there," she said. "Let's go find us someplace to park."

I glared at Toby. We hadn't had that dog one whole

day yet, and already he was acting all stupid around Mama. It would be a miracle if she didn't find out what we had done.

But so far, it seemed like everything was working out good. I'd stolen Willy, no problem. I'd found a good place to keep him. And Mama had a job at a coffee shop that gave her free food. Now all I had to do was stash some of that food in my backpack for Willy.

I took out my notebook and wrote *April 18* in my *How to Steal a Dog* notes. Then I wrote:

Step 5: Things to do after you have stolen the dog:
1. Be sure to act nice to him so he won't be afraid.
2. Play with him some so he will like you.
3. Make sure you put him in a safe place where he won't get wet if it rains.
4. Tie up the rope or string so he can't run away.
5. Find him some food and water.

Uh-oh. Water. I'd forgotten about that. But I was pretty sure that wasn't going to be a big problem. Still, I put a question mark beside that one so I would remember to figure it out.

That night it seemed like I hardly slept at all. A steady rain clattered on the roof and ran down the windows in streams. The inside of the car was so hot I had to crack my window, and then the rain splattered my face and made my pillow wet. I listened to the slow, even breathing of Mama and Toby and thought about Willy. I wondered if he was scared. Was he getting wet? Was he hungry?

Every time I closed my eyes, I could see his freckly face and those shiny black eyes. I could see him cock his head at me and wag his whole body the way he did.

"Don't be scared, Willy," I whispered into the still night air.

The car windows were so fogged up I couldn't even see outside. I used my finger to write *Willy* on the foggy glass. I drew a heart around it, then wiped the window clean and turned my mind to "off."

When I opened my eyes the next morning, I felt all fluttery and excited like on Christmas morning. Today was the day we would find the reward sign for Willy.

Mama made us use the water in the cooler to brush our teeth. While she was putting on her lipstick and stuff in the car, I filled an empty soda bottle with water and put it in my backpack. Then I checked to make sure I had the bag of food scraps for Willy. Yep, half a doughnut and some scrambled eggs.

I pulled Toby close and whispered, "We gotta look for the reward signs today, okay?"

He nodded. "Okay."

I could hardly keep myself from grinning as we made

our way through the streets of Darby on the way to school. I sat up straight and pressed my face against the window, searching every telephone pole we passed.

As we got closer to school, my excitement began to fade to disappointment. I guess in my heart I'd known it was probably too soon to find any signs. We'd only stolen that dog the day before. But in my mind, I had pictured signs on every pole. There they would be, up and down the streets of Darby. In big letters: REWARD. Then there would be a picture of Willy, cocking his head and staring out at the world through his furry black eye patch.

But what I saw outside the window that day was nothing like what I had seen in my mind. There wasn't one single sign. None. Nowhere. I tried to swallow my disappointment and tell myself to be patient. The signs would be up after school, for sure.

"Y'all go straight on back to the car after school, okay?" Mama said, pulling over to the curb.

"We will," I said.

"And stay there, Georgina."

"We will."

"And help Toby with his homework."

I nodded and watched her drive away, then I grabbed Toby's arm.

"Did you see any signs?" I said.

"Nope."

"Dern." I stamped my foot.

"Maybe that lady doesn't care about Willy," Toby said.

I shook my head. "No way. She cares," I said. "Who wouldn't care about a dog like that?"

Toby shrugged. "Maybe she hasn't got any money," he said.

"She *owns* that whole street, Toby," I said.

A school bus had pulled up and kids came pouring out and rushing toward the front door of the school. Me and Toby pushed our way through and went inside.

"Listen," I said. "Meet me at the flagpole after school. We got to take that food over to Willy. Then we can look for the reward signs. I bet they'll be up by this afternoon."

"Mama said we had to stay in the car," Toby said.

I rolled my eyes. "She won't even know what we do. She'll be in the coffee shop."

I watched Toby walk away from me as he headed toward his class. His clothes were all wrinkled and his hair was long and tangled. He was sure a pitiful sight. I wondered if that was how I looked.

When Mr. White asked me for the millionth time if I had given those letters to my parents, I lied again. I said I had, but Mama and Daddy were real busy working and all. I told him my daddy was going to call him any day now. *Yeah, right,* I thought. That was a good one.

I felt bad lying to Mr. White. He was the nicest teacher I'd ever had. He didn't get mad when my science report had fried chicken grease on it. He hadn't said one word when I didn't have a costume for our play about the Boston Tea Party like all the other kids did. And he let me go to the nurse's office, even when he knew I wasn't one bit sick.

But when he asked me about those letters, what else could I do but lie?

Luanne didn't hardly even talk to me all day. I was wearing the same clothes I had on yesterday, and I thought I saw her make a face when I walked into class that morning. I thought I saw Liza poke her at recess and point at me. I thought I heard my name every time I walked by kids giggling and whispering and all.

So who cares, I told myself. I didn't care about any of those kids anymore. Maybe not even Luanne. I found myself doing stuff I never would have done before we started living in a car. Stuff that I knew would make kids poke each other and laugh at me. Like, I took Melissa Gavin's half-eaten granola bar out of the trash and put it in Willy's food bag. And when Jake Samson called me a garbage picker, I just kept my mouth shut and went on back to my desk like I didn't care.

After school I waited at the flagpole for Toby; then we headed off toward the old house to check on Willy. Toby kept whining about how his backpack was too heavy and his feet hurt and all, but I ignored him.

I found a plastic margarine tub on the side of the road and wiped the dirt off of it with the edge of my shirt.

"We can use this for Willy's water bowl," I said, tucking it into my backpack.

Toby kept saying, "Slow down," as we made our way up the gravel road. He splashed right through the muddy puddles, not even caring that his shoes were getting soaked and his legs were covered with mud.

But I didn't slow down. I was dying to get to Willy. I needed to see him. I sure hoped he was okay.

As soon as I rounded the corner of the house, I heard a little yip from the back porch. Then I saw Willy poke his head through the torn screen door, and my heart nearly leaped right out of me, I felt so glad to see him.

Right away, he started wagging his whole body like he was the happiest dog on earth.

"Hey there, fella," I said, sitting on the top step of the porch and giving him a hug. He licked my face all over.

"Are you hungry?" I said. Before I could even open the bag of food, he was pushing at it with his whiskery nose.

"Here you go." I opened the bag and let him gobble up the eggs and stuff inside.

"He sure was hungry," Toby said.

I rubbed my hand down Willy's back while he ate. He was a little wet and smelled kind of bad, but he seemed okay. I opened the soda bottle of water and poured some into the margarine tub.

Willy went to town lapping it up.

"We got to let him run a little bit," I said.

"But what if he runs away?" Toby said.

"We'll keep the leash on him, dummy."

I untied the string from the doorknob. "Come on, Willy," I said.

Me and Toby took turns running up and down the road. Willy ran right through puddles. Sometimes he'd stop and shake himself, sending sprays of muddy water all over me and Toby. Once in a while he stopped to take a good long drink from a puddle. But mostly he just ran and leaped and barked a happy kind of bark. We had to run real fast to keep up with him or else he was liable to bust that string right in two.

"There," I said. "That ought to be enough."

Willy sat in the road in front of me, panting. He lifted his doggy eyebrows and watched me, like he was waiting for something. I knelt down and scratched his ears.

"Don't worry," I said. "You're gonna be going home real soon."

He stopped panting and perked his ears up. Then he put his paw on my knee.

"He sure is cute, ain't he?" Toby said.

"He sure is." I stroked Willy's paw and felt a stab inside. Was it really, *really* wrong to do what I was doing—or was it just a little bit wrong?

I pushed Willy's paw off my knee and stood up. I had to shut those thoughts right out of my head and keep just one thought and one thought only in there. I was doing this for Mama and Toby and me. To help us have a real place to live. Not a car. What was so wrong about that?

We took Willy back to the porch, and I tied the string around the doorknob again.

"Don't worry, fella," I said. "You'll be home soon. I promise."

I filled the margarine tub with water again and set it on the porch beside Willy.

"He needs a bed," Toby said.

I looked at the crummy old back porch. Toby was right. The porch was damp and dirty and covered with sticks and leaves. I should have brought a towel or something to make a bed. I felt another stab inside. I *was* being mean to Willy, wasn't I?

"We'll bring something next time we come," I said. But then I added, "If he's still here."

Toby frowned. "Why wouldn't he be here?"

I sighed. It sure was tiring having to explain every dern little thing to Toby. "We'll be taking him back *home*, you idiot. As soon as we find that reward sign."

"Oh, yeah."

I gave Willy one last pat on the head and made my way down the rotten porch steps. I wanted to look back, but I didn't. I knew I wouldn't be able to stand the sight of that little dog watching me walk away and leave him all alone.

I led the way through the bushes to the road. Behind us, I thought I heard Willy barking.

I don't hear that, I told myself.

I'm not mean, I reminded myself.

This was a good idea and everything is going to turn out fine, I repeated in my head.

I guess I was hoping that if I said those things, then maybe they would be true.

12

"There's one!" I raced across the street.

"Is it for Willy?" Toby called, darting across after me.

I squinted up at the sign nailed on the telephone pole.

"Nope." I sat on the curb and put my chin in my hands. "Another cat."

So far the only signs we'd seen since yesterday had been for lost cats and yard sales.

Toby sat down beside me. "Maybe we should look downtown," he said. "Maybe she didn't put any signs around here."

"Maybe," I said. "But that seems kind of dumb to me. I mean, wouldn't you start in your own neighborhood?"

Me and Toby had been up and down Whitmore Road and nearly every street close by about a million times. There wasn't one single sign for Willy. I just didn't get it. Why wouldn't that lady put up a sign?

"Let's go back over to Whitmore Road one more time," I said.

Toby skipped along beside me, humming. He didn't seem one little bit worried. We'd had Willy for almost two whole days now and I was feeling worse by the hour. My dog-stealing plan had seemed so good when I'd first thought of it. Everything had gone just perfect in my head:

We steal the dog.

We find the sign.

We take the dog home.

We get the money.

The end.

But now things didn't seem to be going so perfect.

When we got to Whitmore Road, I turned to Toby. "Remember," I said, "act normal. Don't look guilty or anything."

"Okay."

We strolled along the edge of the road, looking at fence posts, telephone poles, anything that might have a sign on it. And then we heard someone calling from behind us.

"W-i-l-l-y!"

Toby looked at me all wide-eyed. "What should we do?" he whispered.

Before I could answer, that fat lady was walking toward us.

"Hey," she called to me and Toby.

"Uh, hey," I said, and set a smile on my face.

Her shorts went swish, swish, swish as she walked. A bright pink T-shirt stretched over her big stomach. Even her feet were fat, bulging over the sides of her yellow flip-flops.

"Have y'all seen a dog?" she said. She was breathing hard and clutching her heart like she was going to fall over dead any minute.

"Nope!" Toby practically yelled.

I glared at him, then turned back to the lady. "What does it look like?" I said, squeezing my eyebrows together in a worried way.

"He's about this big." She held her hands up to show us. "He's white, with a black eye patch. And his name is Willy."

Then she started crying. Real hard. Like the way little kids cry.

"I'm sorry," she said, swiping at tears. "I just can't even imagine where he could be."

"Maybe he ran away," Toby said.

Before I could poke him, the lady said, "No, not Willy." Her face crumpled up and she had another full-out crying spell.

I like to died when she did that. And then, as if I wasn't feeling bad enough, she said, "What if something bad's happened to him?"

Before I could stop myself, I said, "You want me and Toby to help you look for him?"

She sniffed and nodded. "Would you?"

"Sure." I poked Toby. "Right, Toby?"

He nodded. "Yeah, right," he said.

The lady smiled and pulled a tissue out of the pocket of her shorts. She blew her nose, then stuffed the tissue back in her pocket. Strands of damp hair clung to her splotchy red cheeks.

"Do y'all live around here?" she said.

Me and Toby looked at each other.

"Uh, sorta," I said. "I mean, yeah, we live over that way." I pointed in the direction of the street where our car was parked. That wasn't lying, right?

"I live right there." She pointed to her house. "I'll show y'all Willy's picture, okay?"

Me and Toby followed her up the walk to the house. At the door, she turned and said, "My name's Carmella, by the way—Carmella Whitmore."

"I'm Georgina," I said. "That's my brother, Toby."

"I'll be right back," she said, then disappeared into the darkness of the house.

I pushed my face against the screen and peered inside. My stomach did a flip-flop. I pressed my face closer to the screen to make sure I was seeing right. I was. The inside of that house wasn't one little bit like I'd imagined it would be. Ever since I'd first laid eyes on 27 Whitmore Road, I'd pictured rooms with glittering crystal chandeliers and fancy furniture. I'd imagined a thick, silky carpet covered with roses. And paintings on the walls. Those fancy kind with swirly gold frames like in museums. I'd even pictured a servant lady bringing in tea and cookies on a silver tray.

But what I saw when I peered through that door was a dark and dreary room filled to bursting with all kinds of junky *stuff*. Piles of newspapers and clothes, boxes and dishes. No chandeliers. No fancy furniture.

Carmella came out of a back room carrying a small silver picture frame.

"Here's Willy," she said, joining me and Toby on the porch and handing me the picture.

There was Willy, looking out at me from that silver frame, smiling his doggie smile.

"He sure is cute," I made myself say, but my voice came out real quiet and shaky.

Carmella nodded and wiped at tears. "He's the cutest dog you ever saw," she said. "And smart? Talk about smart!"

She smiled down at the picture in my hand. "He can count. Can you believe that?"

"Really?" Toby said.

Carmella nodded. "Really. With his little paw. Like this." She pawed the air with her hand.

"Maybe he got lost," Toby said.

Carmella shook her head. "Maybe. But it's just so

unlike him. He knows this neighborhood real good. And everybody knows him." She took the picture from me and dropped into a rocking chair.

"I can't figure out how that front gate got open," she said.

"Maybe the paperboy or something," I said.

"Naw, he just flings it up here on the porch." She looked out at the street. "I've driven everywhere I can think of. I called the animal control officer. I talked to all my neighbors. I just don't know what else to do." Then she started crying real hard again, and I had to look down at my feet. I could feel Toby fidgeting beside me.

"Why don't you put up some signs?" I said.

Carmella looked up. "Signs?"

"Yeah, you know, lost-dog signs."

"Well, stupid me," she said. "Of course I should put up some signs."

"Me and Toby can help," I said. "Right, Toby?"

"Right." Toby grinned at Carmella.

"That would be great," she said, pushing herself out of the rocking chair with a grunt. "Y'all want to come inside?"

Toby looked at me with wide eyes. We weren't supposed to go in anybody's house unless we knew them real good. But Carmella seemed okay to me.

"Sure," I said. "Come on, Toby." I pulled on Toby's T-shirt.

When we got inside, I looked around to see if

Carmella's house was really as bad as it had looked from out on the porch. It was. A big lumpy couch covered with a bedspread and piled with clothes and newspapers. A coffee table littered with soda cans and dirty dishes. A card table with a half-finished jigsaw puzzle. Shelves built into the wall were jammed with ratty-looking books, piles of papers, an empty fish tank, and a bowling trophy. Instead of the rose-covered carpet I had pictured, the wooden floors were bare and worn. And nearly everywhere I looked there was a dog toy, all chewed up and loved. That almost broke my heart and made me tell that lady Carmella everything. But, of course, I didn't. My head was swimming with so many mixed-up thoughts I couldn't get myself to say *anything*.

Carmella shuffled over to a cluttered desk and rummaged through a drawer, then pulled out some paper. She took a red marker out of a mason jar on the desk and stared down at the paper.

"What should I say?" she said.

"How about 'Lost. Little black-and-white dog named Willy,' " I said.

"And then put 'Reward,' " Toby said.

Dern. How come he had to go and say that? I was going to ease into that part, but it was too late now.

"Reward?" Carmella looked kind of confused.

I jumped in there before Toby could. "Uh, yeah," I

said. "That's a good idea. You know, just to make sure people notice and stuff."

"You mean, like, *money*?" Carmella stared down at the paper on the desk.

"Yeah, money," Toby said.

I shot him a look. I wished he'd hush up and let me do the talking.

"Yeah, money," I said. "That would make folks try real hard to find Willy."

"Gosh," Carmella said, "I don't know." She pressed her lips together and kept staring down at the paper on the desk. Then she looked up at me and Toby. "How *much* money?" she said.

"Five hundred dollars," Toby blurted out.

"Five hundred dollars!" Carmella kind of swayed a little bit like she was going to fall right over. "I haven't got *that* kind of money."

"You don't?" I said.

She shook her head.

"Then how much reward *could* you pay?" I said.

"Well, I was thinking maybe, like, fifty dollars?"

Fifty dollars? That wasn't nearly enough. I felt Toby watching me. My mind was racing. But before I could think of what to say, Carmella sank down onto the lumpy couch with a whoosh. Then she shook her head and said, "I guess that's not very much, huh?"

"Well, um, maybe you could get some more," I said.

Carmella looked down at her lap. Little beads of sweat formed on her upper lip.

"I could ask for some extra hours at work," she said. "But that won't help much." Then she snapped her fingers. "I know what! I'll see if I can borrow some money from Gertie."

"Yeah," Toby said. Then he added, "Who's Gertie?"

"My sister."

"Is she the one who owns this street?" I said.

Carmella chuckled. "Lord, no," she said. "She teaches school over in Fayetteville."

"Then who owns this street?" I said. "Your daddy or somebody?"

"What do you mean 'owns this street'?" Carmella frowned at me.

"I just figured since your last name is Whitmore and . . ."

"Oh!" Carmella said. "You mean 'cause this is Whitmore Road?"

I nodded.

Carmella shook her head. "My great-granddaddy owned all this land one time." She swept her arm out toward the window.

"He built this house with his very own hands. Brick by brick," she said. "And had a big ole farm that went way on out there past the highway."

I looked out the window toward the highway. A bad feeling was starting to fall over me. Maybe I'd gotten this whole thing wrong. Maybe Carmella wasn't rich after all.

"What happened to the farm?" I said.

"My granddaddy tried to keep it up, but it just got away from him," she said. "I guess he wasn't much of a farmer." She shook her head as she gazed out the window. "By the time my daddy got this house," she went on, "the only thing left of the family farm was this little ole yard and our name on a street sign."

"Maybe your daddy could give you some money," I said.

"He died eight years ago," Carmella said. "And my mama the year after that. Then Gertie moved away." She looked down at the picture of Willy she was still holding. "All I got is Willy," she said.

With that, she started crying again, and I was feeling so heavy it's a wonder I didn't sink right through the floor.

Suddenly Carmella sat up straight and snapped her fingers.

"You know what?" she said.

Me and Toby waited.

"I *am* gonna call Gertie and borrow some money," she said. "Shoot, I'd pay a million dollars to get Willy back if I had it."

"A million dollars!" Toby said.

She nodded. "Yep." Then she added, "If I had it."

So me and Toby watched her make the first sign:

LOST. LITTLE BLACK-AND-WHITE DOG NAMED WILLY.
$500 REWARD.

I pressed my lips together hard to stop myself from smiling when she wrote that *$500* on there.

This sure was working out good, I thought.

Then we all sat around the coffee table, making more signs. When we had a bunch, Carmella said, "There. That oughtta do it."

"You want me and Toby to put some up now?" I said.

Carmella frowned down at the signs in her hand. "Well, I kind of feel like I ought to wait till I have the money, you know?"

"How long is that gonna be?"

"Not long, I hope," she said. "I'll call Gertie tonight." She looked down at a dog toy on the floor. A chewed-up rubber slipper. She wheezed a little bit as she bent to pick it up.

"I think I'll go drive around some more," she said, turning the slipper over and over on her lap. "I can't hardly stand to think about another night without Willy."

"We'll come back tomorrow, okay?" I said.

Carmella nodded. "Okay."

Me and Toby watched Carmella drive away, then raced back to our car to get some food scraps for Willy. I put a biscuit and half a grilled cheese sandwich in a grocery bag, then rummaged through the stuff in the trunk till I found a towel for Willy's bed.

"Okay," I said. "Let's go."

Willy sure was glad to see us. He wagged and yipped and carried on. When we got up on the porch, he jumped all over us, licking our faces and all.

When I opened the grocery bag with the scraps, he like to went crazy. He gulped everything down, then licked that bag till there wasn't one little crumb left.

I put my arm around him and laid my head on top of his.

"I promise I'm gonna take you home, okay?" I said. I pulled him onto my lap and stroked his back. He laid his head on my knee and sighed.

"He looks kind of sad," Toby said.

I looked down at Willy. "Don't be sad, little fella," I said.

He lifted his doggie eyebrows, and I could see what he was thinking right there on his face. Then the tears that I'd been trying to hold back for so long came spilling out.

"What's the matter, Georgina?" Toby said.

How could I answer that? Should I start with that big red F at the top of my science test today? Or should I just jump right on into how mean our daddy was to leave us in this mess? And then should I move on to how bad it felt to live in a car while my best friend went to ballet school with somebody better than me? Then I could add the part about Willy. How here we were with this cute little dog who never hurt anybody and now he was all sad and probably scared, too? And then there was Carmella, crying and missing her dog so much? And right in the middle of this sorry mess was me, the sorriest person there ever was.

When Mama got off work that night, we drove over to Wal-Mart. I waited in the car while her and Toby went inside. I pulled out my notebook and read my notes on *How to Steal a Dog*.

It sure sounded easy when I read through it. I turned to a fresh page and wrote: *April 20.*

Step 6: When you find some signs about the lost dog, take him back to his owner, get the money, and you are done.
BUT

I drew a big circle around the word *BUT*. Then I wrote:

If there are no signs, you will have to find the owner of the dog and help them make some signs.

While you are doing that, you will have to practice look-
ing nice and not like a dog thief.

Remember to take real good care of the dog so he won't be
hungry or sad or anything.
THEN

I circled the word *THEN* and under that I wrote:

You will have to wait and see what happens next.

I stared down at my notes. I read the last sentence
out loud.

After thinking and worrying half the night, I decided
that's what I'd do, just wait and see what happened next.

13

I don't know what made me do it. I just couldn't stop myself. I watched Toby walk down the hall and into his classroom, and then I turned and went right back out the front door. I hurried up the sidewalk and ducked around the side of the school building. When the buses pulled away from the curb and all the kids had gone inside, I started running and didn't stop till I was way on up toward the highway. My backpack bounced against me as I hurried along the side of the road.

I had to see Willy. I just had to.

I turned down the gravel road that led to the old house. I kept my mind on what I had to do (see Willy) instead of what I had just done (hightailed it out of school).

When I got to the house, I took my backpack off and tossed it on the front porch. Then I pushed through the pricker bushes toward the back of the house. Just as I reached the corner, I heard something that made me stop in my tracks. *Singing.* Somebody was in back of the house, singing!

I jumped into the bushes and ducked down, my heart pounding like nobody's business.

The singing stopped. I held my breath. A man's voice called out, "Are you scared of me or should I be scared of you?"

I knelt in the damp earth and squeezed my eyes shut. My thoughts were jumping around between being scared and trying to figure out what to do. Maybe I could crawl through the thick brush and back out to the road. I pushed a branch aside and flinched when the sound of rustling leaves broke the silence. Willy let out a bark.

"I ain't scared of a coward who won't even show his face," the man called out toward the bushes.

I lifted my head the tiniest little bit to peer through the leaves. A man was sitting on a log beside the back porch! I ducked down. I tried to crawl away from the house toward the path to the road, but a tangle of wild blackberry bushes blocked the way.

"This your dog?" the man called.

I scrambled to think what to do. Should I jump up and run? Should I call out something?

"Me and this dog are just sittin' here sharing sardines," the man said. "You want some?"

I pushed some branches down and peered out. Sure enough, there was Willy, sitting on the bottom step of the porch, licking a paper plate. The man stood up and walked a few steps in my direction. I ducked back down.

"I reckon you and me must think alike," he called toward the bushes. "Never drop your gun to hug a grizzly bear, I always say."

I crawled a few feet along the ground, trying to get a better view of the man.

"But you don't have to worry, 'cause I ain't no grizzly," he said. "You think this little ole dog here would eat sardines with a grizzly?"

Then for the second time that day, I just up and did something without thinking. I stood up, pulled the branches aside, and said, "His name is Willy."

The man looked in my direction. "Well now, I do declare," he said. "I sure am glad you ain't a grizzly, neither."

I stepped out of the bushes and Willy started wagging his tail and kind of prancing with his front legs. The man chuckled.

"Now *that's* some tail waggin' if I ever saw it," he said.

Part of me was saying, *Georgina, stop what you're doing and get on out of here.* But I never was too good at listening to my own self, so I just stood there and checked things out.

The man had nailed one end of a blue tarp to the side of the house and tied the other end to a tree to make a shelter. A ratty sleeping bag was stretched out on the ground beneath it. Leaning against the porch was a rusty old bicycle with a wooden crate strapped on the back. An American flag dangled from the end of a long, skinny pole duct-taped to the crate.

The man gestured toward the bike.

"Easy to park and don't need gas," he said.

He grinned and I caught a glimpse of a shiny gold tooth right in the front. When he gave Willy a pat on the head, I noticed he had two fingers missing. I'd never seen anybody with two fingers missing before.

He must have seen me staring at his hand, 'cause he said, "Got in a tussle with a tractor engine one time." He wiggled his three fingers at me. "Tractor won," he said.

I blushed and looked away.

"My name's Mookie," the man said, tipping his greasy baseball hat.

"*Mookie?*"

He grinned again. "Real name's Malcolm Green-bush, but my mama called me Mookie when I was just a little thing and I been Mookie ever since."

"Oh."

"You got a name?"

"Georgina," I said. "Georgina Hayes."

He stuck out that three-fingered hand of his for me to shake. I confess I didn't feel too good about shaking a three-fingered hand, but I did it anyways.

"I don't mean to go prying into your business, Miss Georgina," Mookie said. "But how come you got your little dog all holed up here in this old house?"

Uh-oh. I hadn't been ready for *that* question. I had to think fast.

" 'Cause we got a new landlord and he says we can't have a dog anymore, so my mama is looking for a new place where we *can* keep a dog, so I'm keeping him here till she finds one," I said. There. That sounded pretty good.

Mookie's bushy eyebrows shot up. "That so?" he said.

"Yessir."

"Well, I can tell you that dog was hungry enough to eat the south end of a northbound skunk."

I looked at Willy. He sat on the step and pawed the air with one of his little paws. Then he yawned, curling up his little pink tongue. I sat beside him and pulled him onto my lap.

"I bring him stuff to eat every day," I said.

"That so?"

Something about the way he said "That so?" made me squirm.

"Except today," I said. "Today I forgot."

"Well then, it's a good thing I had them sardines." Mookie gathered up the paper plate and empty cans and put them in a plastic grocery bag. Then he turned to me and said, "Ain't it?"

I felt squirmy again. "Yessir."

"Seems kind of a shame to keep a little dog like that tied up all the time."

I looked down at Willy and ran my hand along his back. "You wanna run a little bit, fella?" I said.

His head shot up off my lap and he whined.

Mookie chuckled. "I think that's a 'yes,' " he said.

I untied the string leash from the back porch, and Willy leaped off the steps, jumping up on me and yipping like crazy. I took him around to the gravel road, and off we went. Willy looked like he was ready to bust wide open with the pure joy of running. We raced up and down the road a few times till I finally collapsed right there in the dirt, gasping for breath. Willy sat beside me, panting.

"I don't know which he needed more," Mookie called from the side of the house. "Them sardines or that run."

I pulled Willy onto my lap and put my arm around him. He licked my face and then nudged me with his nose.

Mookie strolled out to the road where me and Willy were sitting. "He sure is a smart little fella," he said. "You had him long?"

"Uh, kind of."

"Guess it's pretty easy to love a dog like that." Mookie picked up a piece of gravel and hurled it into the trees. A loud thwack echoed through the woods.

"I bet you miss him a lot," he said. "I mean, you know, not having him in that apartment of yours."

I nodded, stroking Willy's head and trying to keep

my face from looking as squirmy as my insides were feeling.

Mookie hurled another rock into the woods. "I had me a dog when I was a boy," he said.

"What kind?"

"Oh, just a little ole half-breed," he said. "Uglier than homemade soap, that dog was. And dumb? My daddy used to say he didn't have both oars in the water." He chuckled. "But, lawd, me and him was closer than white on rice." He shook his head. "I sure did love that dog."

He reached down and scratched the top of Willy's head. Willy gave Mookie one of those doggie smiles of his.

"Dogs are just like family, ain't they?" Mookie said.

I looked at Willy, and no matter how hard I tried not to, I kept seeing Carmella's sad face and hearing Carmella's heartbroken voice.

I stood up and brushed the dirt off my jeans.

"Where do you live?" I said.

"Yesterday, today, or next Thursday?" Mookie grinned, making his gold tooth glitter in the sunlight.

"Well, um, yesterday, I guess."

"Over there." He jerked his head and kind of rolled his eyes.

"Over where?"

"Over there where I was."

"In a house?"

"A house?" he said real loud, like I was crazy to ask that. "Naw."

"Then where?"

He opened his arms wide and said, "Out here. Outside."

"Outside?"

Mookie nodded. "Yep."

"How come?"

" 'Cause I don't have to paint the air or tar-paper the sky or mop the ground. All I got to do is breathe."

"That's stupid," I said.

Mookie chuckled.

"I better go," I said, leading Willy up the path to the back of the house. Mookie followed along behind us, whistling. I took Willy up to the back porch and tied his leash to the doorknob.

"How long are you staying here?" I said.

"Not long," he said. "I leave my feet in one place too long, they start growing roots."

"Oh." I gave Willy one last pat on the head. "Then, bye." I made my way down the rickety steps. "And thanks for the sardines. For Willy, I mean."

Mookie tipped his hat. "My pleasure."

As I pushed through the bushes toward the front of the house, I had an uneasy feeling. My worries seemed to be piling up, one on top of the other, like bricks on a wall.

I waited in the car until it was time to go back to

school and get Toby. All afternoon, I tried to concentrate on what I had to do next. I went over my *How to Steal a Dog* notes in my mind and thought about how good I'd done so far.

I *had* done good, hadn't I? I mean, I'd found the perfect dog. I'd stolen him. I'd put him in a good place where he was safe. Now all I had to do was wait for Carmella to get the reward money. I bet by the time me and Toby got over to Carmella's, she'd have money, and then I could just move on to the last step in my dog-stealing plan.

Shoot, I bet me and Toby and Mama would be in our nice new apartment just about any day now.

14

Carmella twisted a damp tissue around and around in her lap. Every now and then, she dabbed at her nose.

"I can't hardly stand to face the day anymore," she said. "I couldn't even go to work today."

"How come?" Toby said.

I gave him a nudge with my knee. We sat squeezed together between piles of junk on Carmella's couch. The window shades were drawn. Tiny sparkles of dust danced in a narrow beam of sunlight that slanted across the dark room.

Carmella shook her head. "Gertie says she hasn't got that kind of money, but I know she does."

"Why won't she give it to you?" I said.

" 'Cause she's selfish, that's why."

I watched a fly land on a greasy pizza box on the coffee table. "That's mean," I said.

"She never did like dogs." Carmella blew her nose and waved her hand at the fly.

"What are you gonna do?" I said.

Carmella flopped back against the pillow tucked behind her in the chair. She propped her feet up on a ripped vinyl footstool and rested her hands on her stomach. Then she closed her eyes and made weird little moaning noises.

Toby twirled his finger around his ear, making a sign like Carmella was crazy. I frowned at him and shook my head.

"What are you gonna do?" I repeated a little louder.

Carmella shook her head, making her ripply chin jiggle like Jell-O.

"I just wanna die," she said.

Toby clamped his hand over his mouth like he was trying to stifle a laugh, but I didn't see what was so funny.

"You can't die," I said. "Willy needs you."

Carmella's eyes popped open. She sat up straight and slapped her knee.

"You're right," she said. "Willy *does* need me."

I grinned. "So, what're you gonna do?"

"I'm gonna put those signs up, that's what I'm gonna do," she said.

"The reward signs?" Toby said.

She nodded. "Yep."

"But what about the money?" I said. "Where are you gonna get the money?"

"I'll just be like Scarlett O'Hara," Carmella said.

"Who's that?" Toby said.

"You know, from *Gone With the Wind*?"

I guess me and Toby looked confused, 'cause she went on to explain about Scarlett O'Hara. About how she was this lady in a movie who said "fiddle-dee-dee" and who worried about things tomorrow instead of today.

Then Carmella pushed herself up out of the chair and shuffled over to a rickety card table.

"Will y'all help me put these signs up?" She waved a stack of papers at us. "I made copies with Willy's picture." She smiled down at the signs in her hand.

Toby looked at me and when I said, "Sure," he said, "Sure."

Carmella gave us a little box of tacks and then grabbed her purse and car keys.

"Come on," she said. "Let's go."

Carmella drove, and me and Toby jumped out at every corner to tack a sign up. Toby was scared Mama was gonna see us when we got near the coffee shop, but I told him to hush up and stop worrying. Of course, I knew he was right. She *might* see us. But I had so many other things weighing me down that I didn't have room in my worried mind for Mama. With every sign I put up, that question that I'd been trying to push away kept popping back at me. The question was this: *What in the world are you doing, Georgina?*

By the time we were done, it seemed like there wasn't one street in Darby that didn't have a sign tacked up somewhere. On nearly every corner, Willy's face gazed out at the world with his head cocked in that adorable way of his. It like to broke my heart to look at it.

"I feel better already," Carmella said when we turned onto Whitmore Road and into her driveway. "I have this feeling in my bones that my little Willy is gonna be coming home any minute now."

"But what about the money?" I said.

Carmella flapped her hand at me. "Oh, fiddle-dee-dee," she said. "I'll worry about that tomorrow."

When Mama got off work that night, she drove us over to the Pizza Hut and told us to go on in and wash up. Then we sat in the parking lot and ate corned beef sandwiches and dill pickles. Mama seemed real happy and excited, going on and on about how she's making all kinds of money. She showed me and Toby an envelope stuffed with dollar bills.

"I'm stashing this under the spare tire in the trunk," she said. "But it's just for emergencies, okay?"

"Is that enough to pay for an apartment?" I said, pulling the fat off my corned beef and tucking it into a napkin for Willy.

"Not quite," she said. "But it won't be long now."

"How long?" I popped a piece of chewing gum in my mouth.

"Not long," Mama said.

"*How* long?"

"Not long," Mama said in a mean voice.

"Yeah, right." I rolled my eyes and pulled chewing gum in a long, stretchy string out of my mouth.

Mama whipped around to face me. I stuck my chin up and looked her square in the eye, twirling my gum around like a jump rope.

She turned back around and slumped low in the front seat.

Toby licked his fingers with smacking sounds and said, "Maybe me and Georgina can get some money."

I like to swallowed my gum when he said that.

Mama looked at him and smiled that real sweet smile like she always seems to have for him but never for me.

"Now, how in the world would you and Georgina get money, sweetheart?" she said.

Here it comes, I thought. I knew Toby was gonna mess up sooner or later. I braced myself for what was going to come next, waiting for Toby to tell Mama about Willy and Carmella and all. I tried to give him the evil eye, but he wouldn't look at me.

"I don't know," he said. "Maybe we could find some."

Mama chuckled. "Wouldn't that be nice?"

"Yeah, Toby," I said. "Be sure and let us know when you find a million dollars on the sidewalk, okay?"

Mama shot me a look, but Toby grinned and said, "Okay."

We finished up our supper, and then Mama drove around looking for a place to park for the night. The car was chugging and rattling and jerking like crazy, but she acted like she didn't even notice.

As we pulled into the parking lot of the Motel 6, I spotted one of Carmella's signs. Suddenly that greasy corned beef in my stomach didn't set too well. I lay down on the seat and curled into a ball. Then I closed my eyes and pretended to be asleep.

Later on, after Mama and Toby had fallen asleep, I pulled out my *How to Steal a Dog* notes. I read through every page. When I got to the part that said: *You will have to wait and see what happens next*, I got out my colored pencils and drew little flowers and hearts all around the edge of the page. Then I used a sky blue pencil to write again:

You will have to wait and see what happens next.

I looked out the window at the Motel 6. Inside the lobby, a man was watching TV and sipping from a coffee mug. A soda machine outside the door sent a flickering red glow across the parking lot.

I wished we could've got a room there. Just for one

night. We could stretch out on a real bed. Take a bath in a real tub. Act like real people. We didn't have school tomorrow, so we could spend all day watching TV and stuff. But Mama had said no.

I looked over at Toby, curled up on the backseat with his head propped against the door. I hadn't told him about Mookie yet. I knew he'd get all scared and worried. He'd say we weren't supposed to talk to strangers and Mama would kill us and stuff like that. And I guessed he would be right. But what choice did we have? We couldn't just forget about Willy, could we? We had to feed him and take care of him. Besides, Mookie was probably gone by now. Toby wouldn't ever even know he'd been there.

I closed my notebook and stuffed it back down inside my bag. Then I lay down on the car seat and closed my eyes. No sense worrying about Mookie tonight, was there? I could worry about him tomorrow.

15

Okay, now listen, Toby." I took him by the shoulders and looked him straight in the eye. Then I gave him a little shake just to make sure I had his attention.

"There might be a man back there with Willy." I jerked my head in the direction of the old house.

Toby's eyes got wide. "Who?" he said.

"A man named Mookie."

"A man named Mookie?"

I nodded. "But it's okay," I said. "He's nice. He gave Willy some sardines."

"What's he doing back there?

I shrugged. "Just, like, kinda living there, I guess."

Toby glanced nervously at the house. "How'd he get in?"

"Not *inside*," I said. "He's living *outside*. Out in the back where Willy is."

"You mean like a bum?"

I kept my hands on Toby's shoulders and made him

face me so he'd pay attention. "Look, Toby," I said. "He's liable to be gone. But just in case he's there, don't be scared, okay?"

"Okay."

I dropped my hands from Toby's shoulders and started toward the house.

"Hey, wait a minute," Toby said, grabbing the back of my T-shirt. "How do *you* know about that man named Mookie?" He stamped his foot on the gravel road. "You came here without me."

"I had to," I said.

"When?"

"Yesterday."

"Yesterday?"

I put my arm around him and gave him a little jiggle. "Look, Toby, I just did it without thinking 'cause I needed to see Willy. I'm sorry, okay?"

Toby looked down at his feet. I jiggled him again.

"Okay?" I said.

Finally, in a little tiny voice, he said, "Okay."

"I won't do it ever again."

"Pinkie promise?" he said.

I crooked my pinkie at him. "Pinkie promise."

We linked pinkies, then headed toward the house. I sure hoped Mookie was gone.

We hadn't even got to the corner of the house before Willy started barking.

"It's me," I called out, "Georgina."

"And Toby," Toby called from behind me.

When I rounded the corner, the first thing I saw was that blue tarp. Underneath it, Mookie was stretched out on top of his sleeping bag, his hands folded on his stomach and his hat over his face.

From over on the back steps, Willy wiggled his whole body and let out a bark like he was saying hello.

Mookie didn't move.

"Mookie," I said kind of soft-like so I wouldn't scare him.

Nothing.

"Mookie?" I said a little louder.

Still nothing.

"Is he dead?" Toby whispered.

Suddenly Mookie let out a snort and jumped, sending his hat flying and making me and Toby grab each other. Mookie slapped a hand over his heart and flopped back down on his sleeping bag.

"You like to scared the bessy bug outta me," he said.

"I brought Willy some stuff to eat," I said, wagging my paper bag in the air.

Mookie sat up and put his hat on. "Me and him's been havin' liver puddin'."

I wrinkled my nose. "What's that?"

"Liver puddin'?" Mookie rubbed his hand in a circle on his stomach. "Some good eatin', that's what. Right, Willy?"

Willy sat on the porch steps and lifted a paw.

Mookie chuckled. "That dog's got good taste." He nodded toward Toby. "Who's he?"

"My brother, Toby."

Mookie got up and held out his three-fingered hand toward Toby. I'd forgotten to warn Toby about that, but for once in his life, he didn't act like a scaredy baby. He shook Mookie's hand like he didn't even notice those missing fingers.

"It's a dern shame about that landlord of yours, ain't it?" Mookie said to Toby.

Toby looked at me and then back at Mookie. "Yessir, it is."

I felt relief flood over me. Toby wasn't going to say something stupid like he usually did.

"I bet y'all sure do miss your little dog, don't you?" Mookie said.

"We sure do," I said.

Toby nodded. "Yessir, we do."

Mookie rolled his sleeping bag up and stuffed it into the crate on the back of his bicycle. "Kinda hard to sleep around him, though, ain't it?"

I looked over at Willy. He looked back at me with his shiny little eyes and his eyebrows lifted up like he was curious as anything to hear what I was going to say.

I shrugged. "Sometimes," I said.

Mookie wiped a plastic coffee mug with his shirttail

and put it into a burlap bag. "He snore like that all the time?" he said.

"Not all the time."

Mookie chuckled and put a few more things inside his burlap bag. Then he tucked it into the crate beside the sleeping bag.

"Are you leaving?" I said. I sure hoped he was.

"Yep."

Good, I thought. Now I could concentrate on what I had to do.

Mookie pushed his bike toward the path leading out to the road.

"What about that?" I said, pointing up at the blue tarp.

"Oh, I'll be back," he said.

Me and Toby watched him disappear around the corner of the house. A few seconds later, the sound of gravelly singing echoed through the woods and faded away.

"Is he a bum?" Toby said.

"I don't know." I sat on the step beside Willy and let him root around inside the paper bag. He pulled out a chunk of bagel and gobbled it down.

"I bet he is," Toby said.

I stroked Willy's head while he ate the rest of the scraps I had brought him. (Except a slice of tomato. He just sniffed that.)

"Don't you think he's a bum?" Toby said.

"How should I know?" I snapped.

"I don't like him," Toby said. "He smells."

"So do you!" I hollered, making Willy jump off my lap and slink away like I'd just smacked him upside the head.

"So do you!" Toby hollered back.

Why was I being so mean to Toby? Maybe I figured if I was mean to Toby, I'd feel better about things. But I didn't.

"Let's go take Willy for a walk," I said.

The next day, Mama made Toby stay at the coffee shop and do his homework over in the corner booth by the kitchen. He had whined and carried on, but it hadn't done him a bit of good.

So now I was finally free to be by myself and figure things out. First, I had to visit Carmella and find out if she had gotten any money from her sister, Gertie.

I hurried up the sidewalk toward Whitmore Road. It seemed like the world had blossomed overnight. Bright pink azaleas. White dogwood. The air smelled sweet, like clover. I had the urge to take my shoes off and run barefoot across the soft green lawns. But I didn't.

When I got to Carmella's, I waited outside the gate. The yard was quiet. Not even any birds at the feeder. For a minute, I wished I could step back in time. Back to the day when Willy had come running around the side of the house, chasing that squirrel. Before I had done what I'd done. But I couldn't, so I made my feet go up on the porch and my hand knock on the screen door.

"Who is it?" Carmella called from inside.

"It's me. Georgina."

I heard her wheezy breathing as she came to unlatch the screen.

"Hey," I said.

"Hey."

I looked down at the floor and said, "Did anybody find Willy?"

Carmella shook her head and sank into her ratty old chair. The TV was on with no sound. One of those shopping shows where some lady tries to get you to buy a great big ring that's not even a real diamond. The lady wiggled her fingers around, making the fake diamond sparkle for the camera.

"What about Gertie?" I said.

Carmella shook her head again. "What am I going to do?" she said in this flat kind of voice that made me feel sort of scared.

I sat on the ottoman across from her. "What did Gertie say?"

"She says she hasn't got the money, but I know good and well she does." Carmella wiped her nose with her hand and stared at the TV. "She says I'm pathetic for getting all worked up over a dog."

"So what are you going to do?"

"I'm thinking I'll just go ahead and offer what I can."

"How much is that?"

Carmella sighed. "Oh, I don't know. Fifty dollars, maybe?"

My stomach went thunk.

"But you put five hundred dollars on all those signs," I said.

"I know." Carmella blew her nose. "Maybe whoever finds Willy won't care about money." She stuffed the tissue into her pocket. "I sure wouldn't," she said. "Would you?"

I shrugged. "Um, well, sort of. I mean, not really, but . . ."

With every word that came out of my mouth, I felt like I was digging myself into a hole, and if I didn't stop, I was going to be so far in I wouldn't ever climb out.

Me and Carmella stared at the TV in silence. Now that lady was dangling a shiny gold necklace in front of the camera. Her bright red lips were moving, and I tried to imagine what she was saying. But my mind was such a mixed-up mess that instead of imagining her saying how wonderful that necklace was, I heard her saying, "Georgina Hayes, what in the world are you doing? Have you lost your mind? You bring that little dog back here this instant."

I looked at Carmella and felt a stab. What in the world *was* I doing? Then suddenly Carmella leaned forward and said, "Will you do me a favor?"

"Sure."

"Will you and Toby go check those woods over there across the highway?"

"What woods?"

"Over yonder." She waved her arm toward the main highway. Toward the gravel road. Toward the old house.

"You'll probably think I'm plumb crazy," she said, "but sometimes I think I hear Willy barking from over there."

Thunk. There went my stomach again.

"Really?" I said.

"I drove around over that way yesterday," she said. "But I thought maybe you and Toby could look, too."

"Okay."

"Course, I think I hear Willy scampering around this house, too," Carmella said. "So I reckon it's just my crazy old mind playing tricks on me."

"Toby's doing homework at my mama's coffee shop," I said. "But I'll go look."

Carmella smiled. "I sure do appreciate everything y'all have done for me."

I shrugged. "That's okay." I started for the door. "Besides, maybe if we do find Willy, Gertie'll change her mind and give us five hundred dollars."

Carmella's smile dropped, and she looked like I'd just told her the sky had turned purple.

"What do you mean?" she said.

"Well, um, I mean, you know, the reward and all?"

"Oh." Carmella looked down at her hands and twisted a button on her shirt. "I guess I thought you and Toby were helping me 'cause you *wanted* to."

"We are," I said. "I mean, we *do* want to. I just thought . . ."

"But I will certainly do my best to make sure you get *paid* for your kindness." Carmella's chin was puckering up and she wouldn't look at me.

Dern, I thought. That hole I'd dug myself into was getting deeper by the minute.

16

As soon as I got to the house, I knew Mookie was back. First, I saw his bicycle propped against the bushes on the side. Then I caught a whiff of something cooking.

He looked up when I came around the corner.

"Hey there," he said.

"Hey." I went straight on over to Willy and gave him the bacon I'd brought.

"I'm glad you brought that," Mookie said. " 'Cause he's been eyeing my Hoover gravy like he was gonna eat it all and then me, too."

I squinted into the pan Mookie held over a small fire in a ring of rocks. A pale gray liquid bubbled and smoked in the pan.

"What *is* that?" I said.

"Hoover gravy," Mookie said. "Want some?"

"No, thanks."

I watched him dip a slice of bread into the watery liquid and eat it. Yuck.

"Where's Toby?" Mookie said.

"Doing his homework with my mom."

"Ain't you got homework?"

I sat on the steps and pulled Willy into my lap. "A little." I picked some burrs out of Willy's fur. "But I don't need help like Toby. He's not very smart."

Mookie sopped another piece of bread in the watery gravy. "Smart ain't got a thing to do with school," he said. "I never went past sixth grade, myself." He ate the soggy bread, then added, "And I'm pretty smart."

He licked his fingers. "Besides," he said, "if you ask me, school's about as useful as a trapdoor on a canoe."

"You can't get a job if you don't go to school," I said.

"Says who?"

"Says everybody."

"I work every day of my life," he said.

"Where?"

"Everywhere."

"Like where?" I said.

"Everywhere," he repeated.

I frowned down at Willy and ran my finger over the velvety fur on his nose. Mookie was crazy. Why was I even talking to him?

"Then how come you live like a bum?" I said. I felt my face burn. I shouldn't have said that.

But Mookie just laughed. "I said I worked. I didn't say I got paid."

"You work for free?"

"Sometimes." He took the pan off the fire and scooped dirt over the flames.

"How come?" I said.

He tied the end of the bread bag in a knot, then leaned back against his rolled-up sleeping bag.

"Why not?" he said.

"What kind of work do you do?"

"Whatever I come across that needs to be done," he said. "Might be fixing a roof. Might be painting. Might be digging ditches." He wiggled his three-fingered hand at me. "Might even be fixing tractor engines," he added.

"For free?"

"Sometimes yes. Sometimes no." He took a toothpick out of his shirt pocket and stuck it in the corner of his mouth.

"But why would you do that stuff for free?"

" 'Cause sometimes people need stuff done more than I need money," he said.

That sounded crazy, but I didn't say so. It looked to me like he could use some money.

Mookie took his baseball hat off and scratched his fuzzy gray hair. "Besides," he said, "I got a motto. You wanna hear it?"

I shrugged.

"Sometimes the trail you leave behind you is more important than the path ahead of you." He put his hat back on. "You got a motto?" he said.

I shook my head. "Nope."

He stuck his finger in the gravy. "Okay, little fella," he said to Willy. "It's cool enough for you now." He slid the pan toward the steps, and Willy ran down and lapped up the gravy. Clumps of gooey flour stuck to the bottom of the pan, and he licked them, too.

Then Mookie took me by surprise when he said, "Ain't your mama found you a new place to live yet?"

"Not yet," I said. "But she's working on it."

"You know, I saw the strangest thing today," Mookie said. "I saw a little ole sign with a dog looked just like yours."

I swear, when he said that, my heart sank right straight down to my feet.

"Like Willy?"

Mookie nodded. "Yep."

I couldn't even look at Mookie.

"And you know what was even stranger?" he said.

I swallowed hard and made myself say, "What?"

"That dog's name was Willy, too." Mookie grinned at me, flashing that gold tooth of his. "Ain't that something?"

I looked down at Willy, still licking the pan. "Yessir," I said, surprised at how my voice came out so low and shaky.

Mookie switched the toothpick over to the other side of his mouth and chewed on it.

I looked down at the ground and traced circles in the

dirt with the toe of my shoe. I never thought I'd say it, but I wished I was back in our ratty old car, snuggled up in the backseat, hugging my pillow.

"I better go," I said, giving Willy a quick pat on the head. "Bye now."

I felt Mookie's eyes on me as I walked toward the side of the house. Just as I was about to round the corner, he called out, "Hey, Georgina . . ."

I stopped.

"I got another motto," he said. "You wanna hear it?" He didn't even wait for me to answer.

"Sometimes," he said, "the more you stir it, the worse it stinks."

I turned and hurried up the path to the road.

When I got back to the car, I took out my purple notebook. I slouched down and propped my feet up on the dashboard. I opened to *How to Steal a Dog*.

April 25, I wrote. *Step 7*.

I stared out the window, tapping the pencil against my teeth. I looked down at the paper and wrote:

Remember

I looked out the window again, then back at the paper.

I drew a box under the word *Remember*. Inside the box I wrote:

Sometimes, the more you stir it, the worse it stinks.

Then I closed my notebook, climbed into the back-seat, hugged my pillow, and waited for Mama and Toby.

17

I knew my day was going to be bad when Kirby Price called me a dirt bag in gym and everybody laughed. (Even Luanne. I saw her.) And then it got worse. When Mama got off work that night, the car wouldn't start. She turned the key and there was just one little click and then nothing.

"Well, that's just great," she said, pounding her fist on the steering wheel.

Me and Toby looked at each other, but we both knew better than to say anything.

She turned the key again. Click.

She flopped back against the seat and said a cuss word.

Toby giggled and I poked him to be quiet.

"My life just goes from bad to worse," Mama said.

Then she sat there staring out the window at the Chinese restaurant across the street. A family came out. A *real* family. A mom, a dad, two kids. They broke open their fortune cookies and read their fortunes out loud while they walked to their car. They all smiled and laughed and acted like they had the best life in the world. When they drove by us, they were still laughing. They didn't even look at us sitting in our car that wouldn't start. I wished I was one of those kids, eating my fortune cookie and laughing with my family.

Mama turned the key again. Click.

I stared out the window, praying that old car would start. And then I couldn't hardly believe my eyes. There was Mookie, pedaling his bike up the road toward us.

I ducked down real quick and motioned for Toby to get down, too. Naturally, he had to go, "What?" and sit there looking stupid. I grabbed his T-shirt and yanked him down.

Then I peeked out the window. Mookie had gone on past us and disappeared around the corner.

Mama turned the key again. Click.

I finally got up the courage to say, "What're we gonna do now?"

I held my breath, hoping she wasn't going to yell at me, 'cause I didn't need that after that dirt bag stuff at school.

Mama shook her head and let out a big whoosh of a sigh that blew her hair up off her forehead.

She turned the key again. Click.

"I guess we're sleeping here tonight," she said.

I looked around us at all the places where there were people who would see us. The Chinese restaurant. The Quiki Mart. The Chevron gas station.

"What if somebody sees us?" I said.

"Y'all go on over there to the gas station and wash up," Mama said. "I'm going in the Quiki Mart and get us something to eat."

I watched her run across the street, her jeans dragging on the ground.

"What if somebody sees us?" I hollered out the window. But Mama didn't even turn around.

The next morning Mama walked over to the coffee shop to get her friend Patsy to drive me and Toby to school. I like to died when I saw Patsy pull up beside our car, roll down her window, and say, "Come on, y'all."

She had a big poofy hairdo that stuck way up on top of her head and ugly sparkly earrings and a cigarette hanging out of her big red lips. Her car was rustier than ours, with bumper stickers all over the back. MY OTHER CAR'S A BROOM. HONK IF YOU LOVE JESUS. Stuff like that.

I climbed in the backseat and slouched down as low as I could. *Please don't let anybody see me*, I prayed. *Especially Kirby Price*.

Just before we got to school, Patsy said, "Look at that!"

Me and Toby looked where she was pointing.

There was Mookie, pedaling along the side of the road on that rusty ole bike of his, the little American flag waving in the breeze.

"I've seen that man all over town," Patsy said. "He sure looks happy, don't he?"

I slouched back down in the seat and turned my face away from the window. I sure wished Mookie would get on out of Darby instead of hanging around like he was.

"Imagine being that happy when all you got in the whole world is a beat-up old bicycle," Patsy said.

When we passed him, she waved out the window and hollered, "Hey."

Mookie tipped his hat.

After school, me and Toby had to walk back to the car. It took forever and Toby kept griping and hollering, "Wait up, Georgina."

Then he kept asking, "When are we gonna take Willy back to Carmella's?"

I pretended like I didn't hear him. Finally he grabbed my backpack and yanked.

"I *said*, when are we gonna take Willy back to Carmella's?"

I whirled around to face him. "I don't know, Toby, okay?"

I started off up the sidewalk again. Toby trotted along beside me.

"She's looking for him, Georgina," he said.

"I know."

"I bet Willy wants to go home."

"I know."

"Maybe Carmella has some money now. Maybe Gertie gave her some."

I stopped. "Look, Toby," I said. "I've got to figure this thing out. We went to all this trouble to steal that dog, so we might as well get some money out of it, right?"

Toby shrugged. "I guess."

"What do you mean, you guess?" I said. "That's the whole reason we got ourselves into this mess in the first place."

"What mess?"

I started walking again, but Toby grabbed my arm.

"What mess, Georgina?" he said. "Are we in trouble?"

"No, we're not in trouble."

"Then what mess?"

"Look, Toby," I said. "Carmella may not even get any money. If we take Willy back now, we probably won't get anything. But if we wait much longer, well, I don't know . . ."

"What'll happen if we wait much longer?" Toby said. "Georgina, is Carmella gonna call the police?"

"No."

"But what if she does?"

"So?"

"So, we might get arrested. We're kidnappers," Toby said.

"We are not."

"Well, *dog*nappers, then." Toby's face was puckering up like he was gonna cry. "What if we have to go to jail?" he said.

"Shut up, Toby. There's no such thing as dognappers." I hated it when Toby started thinking up stuff I should've thought of. Maybe we *were* dognappers. Maybe we *could* go to jail.

I pictured Willy's face on a milk carton. His head cocked and his ears perked up. "Have you seen me?" it would say underneath. And Carmella would be sitting there at the kitchen table with her Cheerios, looking at Willy and crying her eyes out.

"And what about Willy?" Toby interrupted my thoughts. "Think about him," he said. "I bet he's sadder than anything."

"Shut up, Toby," I said. I sure didn't need Toby heaping more bad feelings on top of me like that.

Neither one of us said another word as we made our way along Jackson Road toward the car. Toby kept on finding things on the ground and saying, "Hey, look what I found." A quarter. A cigarette lighter. A pencil.

Then, right before we got to the car, we came to one of those LOST DOG signs with Willy's cute little face smiling out at us. I shut my eyes until we were all the way past it, but I could still feel him looking at me.

When we finally saw the car, Toby darted ahead.

"Hey, look at that," he said, pointing to the ground.

I looked down at a shiny quarter nestled in the sandy roadside next to our car. And then I noticed something else. Tracks in the sand.

Tire tracks.

Bicycle tire tracks.

But Toby didn't seem to notice. He just grabbed that quarter like it was made out of gold.

I shuffled my feet in the sand, making those tire tracks disappear, then I unlocked the door and climbed in the backseat.

Me and Toby stayed in the car all afternoon, eating graham crackers with jelly and playing Crazy Eights. Toby kept asking me when we were gonna take Willy back to Carmella, but I didn't even answer him. I knew that was making him mad as all get-out, but too bad. I didn't want to talk about Willy and Carmella. I didn't even want to *think* about Willy and Carmella. I had this bad, bad feeling that I'd gotten myself into a mess. And it seemed like everything I did stirred that mess up more— stirred it up so much it was starting to stink.

18

By the time Mama got back to the car that night, Toby was asleep and I was finishing up my math homework.

"Hey," Mama said, tossing her purse on the seat and handing me a blueberry muffin.

"Me and Toby stayed here all afternoon like you told us to," I said, peeling the paper from the muffin and taking a bite. It was dry and crumbly, but it tasted good.

"I know that's hard on y'all, Georgina," Mama said. "I promise things will be better soon."

Yeah, right, I said in my head. *I've heard that before.*

But out loud I said, "Have you got enough money saved up yet?"

Mama sighed. "Well, I was doing real good until this dern car decided to up and die on us," she said. "I swear, when it rains, it pours."

"What're we gonna do now?" I said.

She dug through her purse and pulled her car keys out. "I'm trying to find somebody who can fix the car cheap," she said. "Patsy's nephew might take a look at it tomorrow."

She put the key in the ignition and turned it. But this time, instead of that click sound we'd been hearing, the engine whirred and whirred and then started with a roar.

Mama jerked her head around and grinned at me.

"It started!" she squealed.

Toby sat up and rubbed his eyes. "What happened?" he said.

I pumped my fist in the air and let out a whoop.

Mama clasped her hands together like she was praying and hollered up at the ceiling, "Hallelujah, praise the Lord!"

"The car started?" Toby said.

Me and Mama nodded at him and then we all slapped each other a high five.

Mama put the car in gear and pulled into the street. "Let's go find us a place to spend the night before our luck runs out and this thing dies again."

We drove through the streets of Darby, Mama humming, Toby snoozing, and me wrestling with all my crazy thoughts.

First there was Willy, tied up on that rotten old porch instead of curled up next to Carmella. Then there was Carmella, missing her little dog more than anything. And then there was Mookie. How come he kept popping into my swirling thoughts? I wasn't sure. But something about those bicycle tire tracks and this broken-down car starting up like it did had got me to thinking about Mookie. Mostly he just seemed like a crazy old man. But sometimes I wondered if maybe he wasn't as crazy as he seemed.

We spent that night on a dark, quiet street not far from Whitmore Road, which made me think so much about Carmella that I didn't sleep too good. I kept picturing her in my mind, tossing and turning in her bed. She'd probably get up a few times and make sure that little doggie door was open just in case Willy came back during the night. Maybe she'd shine her flashlight up and down the street, whistling and calling his name. She might even think she heard him barking from way off in the woods again and drive her car in that direction, hollering his name out the window. Then she'd come back home all alone and sit on the couch with one of his chewed-up toys in her lap.

When my mind started wandering over to that old house, where little Willy was curled up on that dirty, falling-apart porch, I sat up in the backseat and looked out the window at the moths fluttering around a nearby streetlight. The air smelled sweet, like honeysuckle. I could hear the sound of a creek nearby—that even, ripply sound of water. Every now and then, a bullfrog croaked.

Those noises reminded me of the time me and Luanne camped out in her backyard. We had shined our flashlights up on the ceiling of the tent and told each other our secrets. Which boys we liked. How many kids we wanted when we got married. Stuff like that.

Then Luanne had said we had to tell each other the worst thing we had ever done. She told me how one time her mom had knitted her a sweater and she had hated it so much she threw it in the garbage. Then she told her mom she had left it on the school bus.

When it was my turn, I had told Luanne about the time I wrote a nasty word on my desk at school. When my teacher saw it and hollered at me, I told her Emily Markham had done it. Emily had cried so hard she got an asthma attack and had to go home.

That was it. That was the worst thing I'd ever done.

But not anymore. If Luanne and I camped out and shared our secrets now, I'd have to tell her I had stolen a dog. What would she think about that, I wondered.

I fell asleep that night to the soothing sound of the creek, flowing over rocks and winding through the dark woods somewhere outside the car window.

The next day after school, I went straight on over to Carmella's. Toby had to study for his spelling test at the coffee shop. Mama thought I was trying out for the softball team like Luanne and Liza and everybody. I knew I shouldn't be lying to Mama, but I had to. I needed to find out if Carmella had gotten any money yet.

When I got up on the porch, I could hear Carmella inside yelling.

"Yeah, well, thanks a lot, Gertie." Then there was the bang of the phone slamming down. Hard.

"Carmella?" I called through the screen door.

I heard her shuffling up the hall.

"It's me. Georgina." I squinted through the screen into the dark room. Carmella was standing there with her arms dangling limply at her sides and her hair hanging over her face.

"Carmella?"

She lifted her head real slow and looked at me. Her face was all red and splotchy.

I pushed the screen door open and stuck my head in.

"Can I come in?" I said.

She nodded.

I stepped inside. The house smelled like rotten food or something.

"What's the matter?" I said.

Carmella made her way over to her easy chair and dropped into it with a grunt. Her hair was damp with sweat, sticking to her splotchy cheeks.

"I came home from work early just so I could call Gertie," she said. "I should've known better. She just flat out won't lend me any money."

"Oh."

"I guess she don't remember that time I kept her

kids while she was in the hospital," she said. "Or that time I drove clear out to Gatesville in the middle of the night when her car broke down."

She took a magazine off the pile on the coffee table and fanned herself.

"I guess being sisters don't mean nothing," she said.

"So what're you gonna do?"

She threw her hands up and let them fall on her knees with a slap. "Nothing I can do. If somebody brings Willy home, I'll just have to—hey, wait a minute." She snapped her fingers and grinned at me.

"What?" I said.

"I know who'll lend me money," she said.

"Who?"

"My uncle Haywood."

She pushed herself up out of the chair and went over to the desk. She took a beat-up address book out of the drawer and flipped through the pages.

"There!" She jabbed a finger at the page. "Uncle Haywood. I'm gonna call him."

And so she did. Called her uncle Haywood and told him the whole pitiful story. I'd lived every minute of it, but it like to broke my heart hearing about it like that. When she finished, she said, "Yessir," and "No, sir," and "I will."

By the time she had hung up, she was grinning at me and clapping her hands.

"Is he gonna lend you the money?" I said.

"He sure is." Carmella pushed the damp hair away from her face. "Now all I have to do is hope and pray somebody brings my Willy home," she said.

Suddenly her smile drooped and her eyebrows squeezed together. "Do you think he's okay?"

"Who?"

"Willy," she said. "Do you think Willy's okay?"

"Sure," I said.

"Really?"

I nodded.

Carmella looked out the window. "I hope you're right," she said.

"I bet he's trying to find his way home right now," I said.

Carmella kept staring out the window. "I wonder where he is," she said.

I felt my face burning. I was glad Carmella wasn't looking at me.

"I bet he's, um, oh, probably . . ."

"I hope he's not scared," Carmella said.

I shook my head. "Naw, he's not scared. I mean, I bet he isn't."

"You know, like I said before, if I had a million dollars, I'd give every penny of it away just to get Willy back." She nodded at me. "I really would," she added.

I looked down at the dusty wooden floor.

"Did you get a chance to check those woods over

there?" Carmella said, jerking her head toward the window.

"Um, yeah, a little," I said. "I mean, me and Toby looked in there some but . . ."

"Did you call his name?" Carmella said. "And whistle?"

"Um, sure we did," I said. "We called and called and . . ."

"Georgina." Carmella put her hand on my shoulder. "I'll give you that five hundred dollars and anything else you want if you find him."

I nodded, but I couldn't make myself say anything. I knew if there was ever a time for me to say, "Carmella, I know where Willy is," this was it.

But I didn't.

And I knew my silence was like stirring.

And the more I was stirring, the worse it was stinking.

19

I stared up at the stained ceiling tiles of the school nurse's office, trying to make my stomach settle down. For once, I hadn't lied to Mr. White. I really did have a stomachache. I'd had one ever since I'd left Carmella's yesterday.

I had left her house and gone on back to the car. I knew I should've gone over there and taken care of Willy, but I didn't. I guess I was hoping Mookie would share his liver puddin' again.

When Mama and Toby came back, I pretended like I was doing my homework, but I wasn't. I was writing one word over and over, like this:

Willywillywillywillywillywilly

And then after Mama fell asleep, I didn't tell Toby that Carmella was getting the reward money from her uncle Haywood. I didn't say that now it was time to take Willy back and get that money. I kept it all inside me where my aching stomach was.

Finally, I took out my *How to Steal a Dog* notes. I read all the way through them, starting with *Step 1: Find a Dog* and ending with *Step 7* and the part about stirring and stinking.

I turned to a clean page and wrote: *April 28.* Then I added:

Step 8: If you want to, you can take the dog back and tell the owner that you don't want the reward money after all. Here is what will happen if you decide to do that:

1. The owner will be really happy and she can give the money back to her uncle Haywood.

2. The dog will be happy because he is back home where he belongs instead of on that nasty porch.

3. You will be happy because you won't feel bad about stealing a dog, even though you still live in a car.

4. When you stop stirring, it will stop stinking.

Or

You can take the dog back and
get the reward money like you planned.

THAT

is the decision you will have to make.

I drew tiny little paw prints all around the edges of the page before I closed my notebook and put it away.

And now here I was in the nurse's office, staring up at those ceiling tiles with my stomach aching like anything.

When the bell rang, I told the nurse I felt much better (even though I didn't), and I made my way through the pushing, shoving kids in the hall. Outside, I found Toby, and we headed over to the old house.

The whole way there, Toby kept jabbering on and on about stupid stuff. Like how his teacher had hollered at him for doing math with a pen and how some kid's gerbil got loose and went under the radiator. As usual, he was lagging behind, but I hurried on ahead. I needed to get to Willy fast. I needed to snatch him up and hug him, and then maybe my stomachache would go away.

As we hurried up the gravel road, my thoughts turned to Mookie. I sure hoped he was gone. I didn't need his crazy talk that made me feel so squirmy all the time.

When we got to the house, I left my backpack by the road and pushed my way through the bushes toward the back. I rounded the corner, and the first thing I noticed was that Mookie's big blue tarp was gone. The little clearing where his sleeping bag had been was empty. Just a pile of blackened wood and an empty soda can.

Then suddenly it hit me. Silence. Total silence. No happy little hello bark from Willy. I ran over to the back porch and yanked open the rickety screen door and wanted to die right then and there.

Willy was gone.

I must've looked like a crazy person, racing around that little dirt yard, pushing aside the weeds and bushes and hollering Willy's name. Toby kept saying, "What's wrong, Georgina?" and "What happened, Georgina?" Then he started bawling about Willy being gone, and I hollered at him to shut up.

I ran to the edge of the woods and called Willy's name till my throat ached. The quiet that came back to me felt solid and mean, like a slap across the face.

I hurried back out to the road, not even caring about the briars that were snagging my clothes and scratching my arms. I ran up one side of the road and down the other, peering through the trees and calling Willy's name.

Finally, I stopped and held my aching sides, trying to catch my breath. Then I felt Toby punch me in the arm.

"Willy's gone!" he hollered. "And it's all your fault." He looked all wild-eyed and scared.

"*My* fault?"

"Yeah." Toby stomped back up the road toward the house. I ran after him and yanked the back of his T-shirt to make him stop.

"It's *Mookie's* fault," I said. "*He* took Willy. I know he did."

Toby's eyebrows squeezed together. "Mookie took Willy?"

I nodded. "I bet anything he did," I said. "He's crazy."

"What're we gonna do?"

I sat on the side of the road and put my head down

on my knees. What *were* we gonna do? I didn't have one single idea. Then, just when I was wishing that gravel road would open up and swallow me whole, I heard the chinga-chinga of a bicycle bell.

I looked up and saw the best sight I'd ever seen in all my born days. Mookie was pedaling his rusty old bicycle up the road toward us. And trotting along beside him was Willy, his string leash tied to the handlebars of the bike.

I jumped up and raced toward them.

Mookie stopped the bike and I scooped Willy up in my arms and buried my face in his warm fur. Then I felt a wave of mad sweep over me.

"Why'd you take Willy?" I hollered at Mookie.

"Take Willy?" Mookie's eyebrows shot up. "Well, if that don't put pepper in the gumbo," he said.

"What's that mean?" I glared at him. I wasn't in the mood for his crazy talk.

"Means you better slow your mouth down before you start coming out with such as that," he said.

I pressed my face against Willy. His hair was all matted with mud, and he smelled awful.

"For your information, missy," Mookie said, "I was clear on over there by the shopping center when that dog of yours come running up behind me."

"Oh," I said. I knew I should've said more. I should've said, "I'm sorry."

I should've said, "This dog's not mine."

I should've said, "I stole this dog, but now I'm gonna take him back."

I finally managed to lift my head and look at Mookie.

"Then thanks for bringing him back," I said.

I wanted Mookie to say, "That's okay." But he didn't. He just nodded.

I'd forgotten all about Toby until he suddenly said to Mookie, "Are you leaving?"

Mookie nodded again. "I am," he said.

He untied Willy's string leash and tossed it to me. Then he turned his bike around and pedaled off up the road away from us, leaving a wobbly tire track in the dusty road behind him.

And in that instant, I knew I'd been wrong about Mookie. Well, maybe not totally wrong. He *was* kind of crazy. But I guess he was nice, too. And smart. And someone who leaves a good trail behind him.

"Mookie!" I called after him. "Did you fix our car?"

But he just kept pedaling away from us. Then, right before he rounded the curve and disappeared from sight, he gave a little wave with his three-fingered hand.

Suddenly the woods seemed quieter than they ever had before. Not a bird chirping. Not a leaf rustling. Just silence.

"What do we do now?" Toby said.

I looked at Willy, and he cocked his head at me and made me smile.

"We take Willy home," I said.

"When?"

"Tomorrow."

"Yes!" Toby pumped his fist in the air. "Then we get that money, right, Georgina?"

But I didn't answer. I just hugged Willy.

20

I had to admit, Toby had been pretty good at stealing a dog. He had thought of stuff like food and all. He had found the string leash. And best of all, he hadn't goofed up and told Mama what we had done. So I felt kind of bad about taking Willy back to Carmella's without him. I knew he'd be mad as all get-out.

And I knew Mr. White would be mad as all get-out if I missed school again and didn't bring a note from Mama. I knew he'd have a meeting with the principal like he'd warned me would happen. A meeting to talk about me and how much I'd been messing up. A meeting about why my mom wouldn't answer Mr. White's letters and all.

I knew what was ahead of me if I did what I'd planned, but I was gonna do it anyways.

I made sure Toby was in his classroom, then I hurried back outside and raced over to the old house. I couldn't hardly get my feet to go fast enough as I pushed through the bushes on my way to the back.

Please, Willy, be there. Please, Willy, be there, I said over and over inside my head.

As soon as I rounded the corner of the house, I heard Willy's happy little yips.

"Hey there, fella," I called, hurrying over to the porch.

Willy stuck his head through the torn screen and wagged his whole body.

I sat on the step and let him jump through the screen door into my lap.

"How you doin', fella?" I said, scratching the top of his head.

He sniffed my backpack, making little snuffling noises. I pulled out the peanut butter sandwich I had brought him, and tore it into pieces. He gobbled them up, swallowing them whole without even chewing.

"Ready to go home?" I said.

Willy perked his ears up and let out a little bark. That dog sure was smart.

I untied his leash and started for the path that led to the road. But as I was crossing the clearing where Mookie had camped, I noticed something that made me stop. A little green dog collar, lying on top of the log that Mookie used to sit on.

My heart dropped with a thud. That collar looked familiar.

I picked it up and studied the tag. Yep. There it was, plain as day. *Willy*.

I turned it over and read:

Carmella Whitmore
27 Whitmore Road
Darby, NC

I felt a big blanket of shame fall over me. Mookie had found Willy's collar. He had known the truth about Willy. He had known the truth about me.

I looked down at Willy. He was watching my face like he knew every thought in my head.

"Mookie knew about us, Willy," I said.

Willy whined and wagged his tail.

"I wonder why he was so nice to me," I said.

Willy nudged me with his nose.

I buckled the green collar around his neck and said, "Come on, Willy. Let's go home."

By the time I got to the corner of Whitmore Road, Willy was pulling so hard I thought that string was gonna bust in two. I knew he was dying to race up the street, through the gate, up the porch steps, through the doggie door, and right into Carmella's lap. But I needed to slow down a minute. I had to make sure the coast was clear and nobody was outside.

"Hang on, little fella," I said.

I squinted up the road, checking out the yards and driveways.

"Okay, Willy," I said. "Let's go."

I hurried toward Carmella's house. By the time we got to the hedge, Willy was practically going crazy, leaping and carrying on.

I tiptoed along the hedge, trying to keep Willy from yanking the string right out of my hand. I hoped Carmella wasn't home, but when I got to the gate, I could see her car in the driveway. I untied the string from Willy's collar. Then I took his whiskery face in both my hands and rubbed my nose back and forth against his. An Eskimo kiss.

I lifted the latch and opened the gate. Then I let go of Willy's collar and watched him dash across the yard and up the steps, then disappear through the doggie door and into the house.

I turned and hurried back up the road. But the farther I got from Carmella's house, the heavier my feet felt. By the time I got to the corner, they felt like cement bricks, slowing me down until I couldn't take another step.

What's wrong with you, Georgina? I said to myself. *Don't stop now. Get on outta here before somebody sees you.*

But I guess my heart was taking over my feet, making me stop. Making me turn around. Making me walk on back to Carmella's.

I stood outside the gate. Music from a radio drifted out of the screen door. More than anything, I wanted to disappear. To leave Whitmore Road and never come back. To just pretend like I'd never laid eyes on Willy or Carmella.

But I couldn't.

I took a deep breath and put my hand on my heart. I could feel it beating, fast and hard. Then I opened the gate and made my cement feet walk up the sidewalk to Carmella's front door.

"Carmella," I called through the screen.

"Georgina!" Carmella squealed from inside. "Guess what!"

She came to the door carrying Willy. He was licking her face all over and wiggling his whole body.

"Willy's home!" Carmella said. Tears were streaming down her face and she looked about as happy as a person could be. "He just came running right through that doggie door and into the kitchen like he'd never been gone." She kissed Willy's nose. "Can you believe that?" she said.

"No," I said. "I mean, yeah, I *can* believe that, 'cause, um . . ."

"Come on in." Carmella pushed the screen door open. "I'm gonna give him a bath. He's a mess."

I stepped inside.

"But first," Carmella said, "I'm gonna cook him some sausage."

"Carmella . . ." I followed her down the hall and into the kitchen. "I, um, I need to, um . . ."

But Carmella wasn't listening. She was humming and talking to Willy while she put little sausages in a frying pan.

"Carmella," I said louder than I'd meant to, 'cause it sounded like a yell.

She looked at me kind of surprised.

"I need to tell you something," I said.

She put a lid on the pan and turned to me.

"Okay," she said.

I looked down at the dirty linoleum floor. Willy had left little muddy paw prints in front of the stove where Carmella was standing.

"I stole Willy," I said to the floor.

A terrible silence settled over the room. I could hear Carmella's wheezy breathing. In and out. In and out.

Finally, she said, "What do you mean?"

I looked up. She was standing by the stove, holding a fork. Her face was white, making her freckles stand out like sprinkles of cinnamon. Willy sat on the floor beside her, watching her, waiting for that sausage.

"I mean, I stole Willy," I said. "I took him right out of your yard."

Carmella gripped the edge of the counter for a minute, then pulled out a chair and sank into it.

"But why?" she said.

And then I did the hardest thing I'd ever done. I told

Carmella everything. I started with those three rolls of quarters and the wadded-up dollar bills in the mayonnaise jar, and I ended with Mookie leaving Willy's little green collar on that log.

And then I waited for Carmella to hate me.

But you know what?

She reached out and took my hands in hers and didn't sound at all hateful when she said, "I guess bad times can make a person do bad things, huh?"

I hung my head and couldn't get myself to say another word.

"You did a real bad thing, Georgina," Carmella said.

I nodded, keeping my head down so my hair would hide my face. Tears dropped right off the end of my nose and onto the floor.

The room was silent except for the sizzle of the sausage on the stove and the tick, tick, tick of the clock over the refrigerator.

Carmella pushed herself up off the chair and went over to the stove. She took the sausages out of the pan and cut them into pieces. Willy whined at her feet.

Tick, tick, tick went that clock.

"I'm sorry," I said.

Tick, tick, tick went that clock.

Carmella dropped the sausage pieces into Willy's bowl. He gobbled them up and then kept licking the bowl, making it slide across the floor.

"I guess I better go," I said. But I didn't move. I

stayed there with my heavy, cement feet planted firmly on the cracked linoleum of Carmella's kitchen floor, waiting for her to make me feel better.

But she didn't.

So I moved my heavy feet, one in front of the other, down the hall, through the front door, and out onto the porch. I was almost to the gate when Carmella called, "Georgina."

I stopped and turned around.

She stood on the porch holding Willy. His tail wagged, thwack, thwack, thwack against her leg.

"Why don't you and Toby come by tomorrow?" she said. "Y'all could take Willy for a walk."

I felt my whole self get lighter, as if that heavy blanket of shame I'd been wearing had been lifted right up off of me.

I nodded. "Okay," I said. "We will."

Then I hurried out of the gate and up the road. I couldn't wait to tell Toby what I'd done. I knew he wouldn't be mad when I told him how happy Willy was and how Carmella didn't hate us. I'd let him hold the leash when we walked Willy tomorrow, and he wouldn't think I was mean anymore. When I got to the corner of Whitmore Road, I stopped and looked back. Carmella was still standing on the porch, holding Willy like she wasn't ever going to put him down.

She waved at me.

I waved back.

Then just as I was about to turn and head back toward the highway, I glanced down and noticed my footprints in the dirt along the side of the road. I smiled, thinking about Mookie and his motto. About the trail you leave behind being more important than the path ahead.

Then I turned and raced off toward school to wait for Toby.

21

We lived in that nasty old car for two more days. Then one day Mama came back from work and said, "Pack your bags, boys and girls. We're *moving*."

Me and Toby looked at each other, then back at Mama, waiting.

She tossed two Snickers bars into the backseat and said, "You heard me. We're moving. And I'm talking *house*. A *real* house."

Me and Toby started whooping and bouncing up and down on the backseat. Then we took down our beach towel wall and jammed all our stuff into garbage bags. Schoolbooks and dirty T-shirts. Playing cards and comic books.

As we drove to our new house, I felt a flutter of excitement as I thought about being normal again. I pictured myself going to school in clean clothes and having all my homework done and Mama telling Mr. White that everything was fine now, so don't worry about Georgina anymore. I pictured me and Luanne having a sleepover like we used to, painting our toenails and sharing our secrets. Maybe working on our cooking badge for Girl Scouts. I even pictured myself sitting on my very own bed wearing my new ballet shoes, combing my hair so I'd look nice for my ballet lessons with Luanne and Liza Thomas.

When we pulled up in front of our new house, me and Toby grinned at each other. It was a tiny white house with a rusty swing set in the red-dirt yard and a refrigerator with no door sitting right up on the front porch.

But it looked like a castle to me.

Somebody named Louise was already living there with her baby named Drew. Louise was a friend of Patsy's and needed somebody to share the house with her and help take care of Drew and pay some of the rent.

I didn't have my very own room, but I had my very own bed. Louise gave me a plastic laundry basket to keep my things in and told me to put it up on the closet shelf so Drew couldn't get my stuff.

The first night in our new house, Mama brought home pizza and we watched TV. Before I went to sleep, I lay in my bed and stretched my legs out under the cool sheets. The tiny window across the room was open, and a soft breeze lifted the faded curtains. Moths flapped and buzzed against the screen.

I reached under my pillow and took out my glittery purple notebook. I turned to my *How to Steal a Dog* notes, and in the dim glow of the hall light I read through *Step 8* again. About making a decision. About getting the reward or not getting the reward. I smiled to myself when I read the part that said:

> *THAT*
> *is the decision you will have to make.*

I knew I had made the right decision because my tapping insides had finally settled down.

But I still felt bad about what I'd done. I still wished I could turn back the time far enough to where I could do things different.

But at least when I'd gotten to *Step 8*, I'd made the right decision.

I turned to a fresh page in my notebook and wrote: *May 3.*

> *Step 9: Those are all the rules for how to steal a dog.*
> *But*

I drew a red heart around the word *But*. Then I wrote in great big letters:

DO NOT STEAL A DOG
because

I drew a blue circle around *because*. Then I took out my gold glitter pen and wrote:

it is NOT a good idea.
THE END

I closed my notebook and slid it back up under my pillow.

As I lay there in my very own bed, I thought about Mookie. I wondered what he was doing right that very minute. Was he making Hoover gravy? Was he wiggling that three-fingered hand of his at somebody? Was he fixing somebody's car?

Where was he leaving his trail now?

I thought about Willy, too. I bet he was curled up at the foot of Carmella's bed beside his chewed-up toys, dreaming about sardines and liver puddin', happy as anything to be back home again.

I looked over at Toby, sucking his thumb in the bed next to mine. Then I tiptoed over to the window and looked out into the night. I took a deep breath. The air smelled good. Like honeysuckle and new-mowed grass.

It didn't stink at all.

GO FISH

BARBARA O'CONNOR

What did you want to be when you grew up?
For most of my childhood, I wanted to be a teacher. I also thought I might like to be a dance instructor and have my own dancing school, which I actually did for a few years.

When did you realize you wanted to be a writer?
I don't remember ever making a conscious decision to be a writer. Writing was just something that I loved doing from a very young age. I still have boxes and boxes of things I wrote as a child, from poems to stories to plays.

What's your first childhood memory?
The earliest memory I have is when I was about four years old and the ice cream truck was coming through my neighborhood. My sister and all her friends were running after it but I couldn't keep up. I remember just standing there crying.

What's your favorite childhood memory?
Being at my grandmother's house in North Carolina with my cousins. My grandfather had filled an old chicken coop with

sand to make a huge indoor sandbox. We played in that chicken coop sandbox for hours.

As a young person, who did you look up to most?
My dad.

What was your worst subject in school?
Economics. (I'm still not very good at economics.)

What was your best subject in school?
English.

What was your first job?
I used to teach dancing lessons to neighborhood children. I had a dance studio in my garage that my father helped me make.

How did you celebrate publishing your first book?
With lots of whooping and yahooing—and then dinner out with my family.

Where do you write your books?
In the winter, I write in my office, which is a converted bedroom in my house. I have a huge, lovely desk that was handmade by a friend of mine. The wood is beautiful and there is lots of room for family photos. My two dogs always stay in there with me and keep me company.

In the summer, I love to sit out on my screened porch. I love being able to watch the birds and look at the flowers while I write.

Where do you find inspiration for your writing?
My biggest inspiration comes from my memories of my childhood in the South. But I also love to go back to the South and pay attention to all the little things that make it so special there: the

way the people talk and the food they eat; the weather; the trees—all the things that add richness to a story.

I'm also inspired by reading.

Which of your characters is most like you?
Jennalee in *Me and Rupert Goody*. I think I felt the most like her as I wrote her story and I definitely related to the setting of the Smoky Mountains, where I spent a lot of time as a child.

When you finish a book, who reads it first?
I belong to a writers group, so I share bits and pieces of my stories as I write them. But once the story is complete and polished, the first people who read it are my editor, Frances Foster, and my agent, Barbara Markowitz.

Are you a morning person or a night owl?
No question about it: a morning person!

What's your idea of the best meal ever?
Sushi! (But some good ole greasy fried chicken and big, hot, fluffy biscuits sound pretty good, too.)

Which do you like better: cats or dogs?
I am definitely an animal lover. I love them all. But dogs are my favorite. I adore them.

What do you value most in your friends?
A sense of humor, honesty, and respecting my need for "alone" time to recharge my batteries.

Where do you go for peace and quiet?
I like being home. But outside of my home, I love to walk with my dogs, either in the woods or at the beach.

What makes you laugh out loud?
My husband and son both have a great sense of humor, so I laugh with them a lot. My two dogs also make me laugh.

Who is your favorite fictional character?
Beverly Cleary's Ramona Quimby.

What are you most afraid of?
Heights and snakes.

What time of year do you like best?
Summer.

What's your favorite TV show?
Judge Judy.

If you were stranded on a desert island, who would you want for company?
Probably somebody who was very good at building boats out of things you find on a desert island.

If you could travel in time, where would you go?
The fifties. Everything seemed much simpler then.

What's the best advice you have ever received about writing?
Author Linda Sue Park often passes down advice that she got from Katherine Paterson, which is to set a goal of writing two pages a day. That doesn't seem nearly as daunting as sitting down to write a novel.

What do you want readers to remember about your books?
I'd like for readers to remember my characters, since that is the most important part of any story to me.

What would you do if you ever stopped writing?
I'd love to be a librarian, but it's probably too late, since I'd have to go back to school and I'm not sure I'm ready for that anymore. So, I guess I'd just stay home and play with my dogs and work in my garden and figure out a way to pay the electric bill.

What do you like best about yourself?
I'm very organized and always punctual. I also think I have a pretty good sense of humor.

What is your worst habit?
Always needing to plan things instead of being spontaneous. And, well, maybe nagging.

What do you consider to be your greatest accomplishment?
My greatest accomplishment is having raised a good son who is honest and kind. But I'm also pretty proud of having written books.

Where in the world do you feel most at home?
Down South.

What do you wish you could do better?
I wish I could sing and draw better. And I wish I could play a musical instrument.

What would your readers be most surprised to learn about you?
I have no sense of smell and I can eat a whole bag of cookies.

MAVIS JEETER HAS NEVER LIVED IN ONE PLACE
long enough to have a real best friend. Rose Tully is a worrier
who feels like she doesn't fit in with the other girls in her neighborhood. When a runaway dog, Henry, brings the girls together,
all three come to find friendship in places they never expected.

Turn the page for an excerpt
of Wonderland

Sometimes the friends you've always wanted
are found in the most unlikely places

Wonderland

By the author of *Wish*
BARBARA O'CONNOR

MAVIS

Mavis Jeeter sat on the bus stop bench beside her mother and whispered goodbye to Hadley, Georgia. She took a deep breath and let out a big, heaving sigh to send a signal to her mother that she was tired of saying goodbye.

"Why can't we stay here?" she asked every time her mother announced that they were moving.

Then her mother would explain how she was sick of Podunk towns and godforsaken places. How she needed a change of scenery. How she had a friend or a cousin or a boyfriend waiting somewhere else.

This time they were leaving Hadley, Georgia, so her mother could work as a housekeeper for a rich family in Landry, Alabama.

Mavis let out another heaving sigh that blew her

tangled hair up off her forehead. Then she leaned forward and squinted down the road.

"When's the bus coming?" she asked for the umpteenth time.

"Soon," her mother said for the umpteenth time.

Sometimes Mavis wished she lived with her father in Tennessee instead of just visiting him every now and then. Her father stayed in one place. But then, he lived with his mother, who disapproved of Mavis.

"That child runs wild," she complained right in front of Mavis. "Not one lick of discipline from that so-called mother of hers," she'd say, as if Mavis were invisible and not sitting on the couch there beside her. "Lets her run wild," she'd mutter, flinging her arms up and shaking her head.

Finally, the bus came roaring up the road, and the next thing Mavis knew, she was watching Hadley, Georgia, disappear outside the window.

"Goodbye, fourth grade," she whispered when the bus rumbled past Hadley Elementary School. "Have a nice summer," she added.

It was only a few weeks ago that kids had hooted and hollered on the last day of school, but now the window shades were drawn in the empty classrooms.

"So long, Bi-Lo," she whispered when they passed the grocery store where her mother had worked for a few months—until she came home one day and announced, "I'm not asking 'Paper or plastic?' ever again."

"Adios, best friend," Mavis whispered as they drove past Candler Road, where her best friend, Dora Radburn, lived. Then she let out another big, heaving sigh. Actually, now that she thought about it, Dora hadn't really been a best friend. She never saved Mavis a seat at lunch, and she had flat-out lied about her birthday party. Maybe if the Jeeters stayed in one place long enough, Mavis could have a *real* best friend.

So as the bus turned onto the interstate, Mavis said one final goodbye to Hadley, Georgia, and decided right then and there that in Landry, Alabama, she would have a real best friend.

ROSE

Sometimes it seemed to Rose Tully that everything about her was wrong. It also seemed as if her mother reminded her of that nearly every minute of every day.

"Don't slouch, Rose," she'd say.

"You can't wear *that*, Rose."

"Stop slurping your soup, Rose."

But even if Rose sat up straight or changed her dress or sipped her soup as daintily as could be, there would still be something wrong.

And so it was that on a fine summer morning in Landry, Alabama, with the sun streaming through the dining room windows overlooking the garden, Rose plucked raisins out of her oatmeal and waited for her mother to tell her what was wrong.

"Stop *doing* that, Rose," her mother said.

Rose plopped a raisin into her mouth and glanced at her father. Sometimes he would say, "Aw, Cora, cut Rose some slack." But today he didn't. Today he gulped down his orange juice in a way that made Mrs. Tully squint, and then he grabbed his briefcase and hurried out the door without so much as a goodbye.

"Hurry up, Rose," Mrs. Tully said. "There's liable to be traffic on the interstate, and I'm not even sure where the bus station is." She took one last sip of coffee and added, "I'm starting to have reservations about this Jeeter woman if she doesn't even have a car."

"But she's bringing her daughter, right?" Rose said.

"Unfortunately, yes," Mrs. Tully said. "I'm not sure this was one of my better ideas."

Rose folded her napkin and placed it neatly next to her plate. She didn't say it out loud, but she was hoping that this Jeeter woman's daughter was nicer than Amanda Simm.

"Wait for me outside," Mrs. Tully snapped. Then she snatched her napkin off the table, gathered plates and bowls and juice glasses with a clatter, and disappeared through the swinging door into the kitchen, leaving a cloud of discontent behind her.

When Rose opened the front door, a wave of thick summer heat drifted in and mingled with the icy air-conditioning in the foyer. The pleasantly mild days of May had given way to the sultry days of early June, the beginning of a sure-to-be stifling Alabama summer.

Rose's house was the biggest one in Magnolia Estates. It had a winding driveway lined with neatly trimmed boxwoods and a doorbell that chimed Beethoven's "Ode to Joy." On each side of the front door sat a concrete lion, its mouth open in a mighty roar. When the Tullys moved there two years ago, Rose had named them Pete and Larry.

Out on the porch, Rose patted Pete and Larry on the tops of their heads and savored the smell of freshly mown grass. Monroe Tucker, the gardener, had already been there this morning, getting an early start like he always did to beat the midday heat. Because the Tullys' yard was so large, Monroe came three days a week, trimming the boxwoods and weeding the gardens and making sure the azaleas were the exact same height, the way Mrs. Tully liked them.

Rose ran to the end of the driveway and looked up the road toward the gatehouse. She wished she could visit Mr. Duffy instead of going to the bus station with her mother. She wished she could take him some blackberries to try to cheer him up. She wished she could show him how good she had gotten at the magic trick he had taught her. But more than anything, she wished Mr. Duffy's little dog, Queenie, hadn't died.

MAVIS

As they pulled into the bus station in Landry, Mavis's mother went over all the rules again.

Never go into the Tullys' house without knocking first.

Remember to say "Yes, ma'am" and "No, ma'am," because rich people like that.

Don't say anything bad about the garage apartment where they would be living, even if it's a dump.

"And whatever you do," she said, jabbing a finger at Mavis, "be nice to that lady's daughter."

"What's her name again?"

"Rose."

"Rose," Mavis whispered to herself. That was a friendly sounding name.

Okay, *this* time she was not going to beat around the bush.

Rose would be her best friend in Landry, Alabama.

Her mother took a tiny mirror out of her purse and checked her reflection, smoothing her hair and blowing herself a kiss. "Pretty good-looking dame, if I do say so myself," she said, winking at Mavis and tossing the mirror back into her purse. "Okay, May May, let's do this."

Then off she went, strutting up the aisle of the bus like a runway model, leaving Mavis to hurry after her.

ROSE

Rose climbed into the front seat of the Tullys' shiny black car and listened to her mother complain about the heat and about the bad haircut that Darlene Tillman had given her and about Mr. Tully, who never put gas in her car. As they made their way through Magnolia Estates, worry hung over Rose like a thundercloud.

First there was the worry about the vacant lot across the street. In the middle of the lot was a small gold sign with magnolia blossoms around the edges and fancy black lettering that read BUILD YOUR DREAM HOME HERE. Rose wished that people would stop building their dream homes in Magnolia Estates. Before long, there would be no more blackberries to eat or wildflowers to pick or trees to climb. In their place would be big brick houses with tidy lawns kept green all summer by invisible sprinklers that came on in the wee hours of the morning.

When they drove past Amanda Simm's house, Rose's cloud of worry began to grow bigger and darker. Her mother and Mrs. Simm were forever trying to get Rose and Amanda to play together again. But Rose and Amanda weren't very fond of each other anymore. They *used* to play together when they were in third grade, but now that they were going into fifth grade, it seemed as if they had nothing in common. Amanda didn't like tap dancing, and Rose didn't like shopping at the mall. Amanda didn't like playing circus with Pete and Larry, the concrete lions, and Rose didn't like sleepovers. But, for Rose, the icing on the cake was the fact that Amanda didn't seem to like Mr. Duffy, the gatekeeper, anymore. She never actually *said* it, but Rose could tell. Amanda had started making faces when Mr. Duffy told stories about raising pigs in Vermont when he was young. She giggled in a not very nice way when he fell asleep in the gatehouse and delivery truck drivers had to honk their horns. And she rolled her eyes when he pretended to take quarters out of their ears. Now Amanda never went up to the gatehouse anymore, which was fine with Rose.

When the Tullys drove past the gatehouse of

Magnolia Estates, Rose's dark cloud of worry drifted down and settled over her like a blanket of sadness. Mr. Duffy had been the gatekeeper ever since the Tullys had moved there two years ago. He kept a log of who was allowed to come into Magnolia Estates and where they were going. A plumber for the Barkleys on Dogwood Lane. The UPS man delivering packages to somebody on Rosewood Circle. Some ladies playing bridge every other Wednesday at Mrs. Larson's on Camellia Drive.

Mr. Duffy had a way of making Rose feel better about things. He comforted her when she didn't want to go to sleepovers in the Magnolia Estates clubhouse. He knew just the right thing to say when she felt anxious about riding the school bus. And he never made her feel bad if she didn't take flower-arranging classes or piano lessons like her mother wanted her to.

Rose visited him nearly every day. She would tell him about school, and he would tell her about the giant catfish that had jumped clean out of his boat and back into the lake. She would show him the tap steps she learned in dancing school, and he would teach her a magic trick involving paper cups and buttons.

And nearly every day, Mr. Duffy's little dog, Queenie, had waited patiently for Rose to drop graham cracker crumbs or popcorn or maybe even to toss her a piece of cheese. She would bark at the Glovers' cat and take treats from the telephone repairman and waddle out to the edge of the road to watch the trucks bringing bricks for somebody's dream home.

But now Queenie was gone, and Mr. Duffy didn't do magic tricks or play checkers anymore. He didn't play the kazoo while Rose sang "Oh My Darling, Clementine." And he didn't say "Look out, catfish, here I come" when it was time to go home to his tiny trailer out by the lake.

So as the Tullys' shiny black car made its way up the interstate toward the bus station, Rose thought and thought and thought about how she could cheer up Mr. Duffy.

MAVIS

Mavis hopped on one foot around the bus station, careful to only land on the black squares of the linoleum floor. If she touched a white square, something bad would happen, like maybe she would lose that heart-shaped good-luck rock she had found in their yard in Georgia, or her dad would change his mind about letting her spend Christmas with him in Tennessee.

"You're giving me a headache," her mother said, closing her eyes and massaging her temples.

"When are they getting here?" Mavis asked, hopping over to the window and peering into the empty parking lot.

Her mother rummaged through her purse and pulled out another pack of gum. She had been chewing gum constantly for the last three days. Mavis knew that what she really wanted was a cigarette, but Mrs. Tully had been very clear about the no-smoking rule.

"Highfalutin people don't care if they're late," her mother said.

"How do you know they're highfalutin?" Mavis asked.

Her mother popped a piece of gum into her mouth and said, "Believe me, I know."

"So why do you want to work for highfalutin people?" Mavis said.

"In case you haven't noticed, Miss May May," her mother said, "it takes money to get anywhere in this world. If highfalutin people want to give me money for the pleasure of changing their sheets when they're not even dirty or serving them sliced cantaloupe on china plates, I'm willing to give it a shot."

Uh-oh. Give it a shot? That had a *temporary* ring to it. Mavis had hoped that maybe this move to Alabama would be permanent. Or at least till she finished fifth grade. So Mavis decided that she would have to make Rose her best friend right away.

Just then, a shiny black car turned into the parking lot. A lady and a girl got out and walked toward the station.

The lady wore a flowered skirt and a ruffly white blouse. Tucked under her arm was a tiny purse the same color as her shoes.

Mavis was surprised to see that the girl wore a skirt, too. Why would a kid wear a skirt in the summertime? The girl's mousy brown hair was pulled neatly into a ponytail tied with a purple ribbon. Mavis's mother had said the girl was the same age as she was, but this girl looked younger, short and skinny and practically running to keep up with her mother, who marched across the parking lot toward the door of the bus station.

Mavis's mother quickly took the gum out of her mouth and stuck it under one of the plastic seats in the station. She smoothed her hair and brushed doughnut crumbs off her shorts and reminded Mavis for the gazillionth time to say "Yes, ma'am" and "No, ma'am." Then she set a smile on her face and called out, "Mrs. Tully! Over here!"

Mavis watched that highfalutin woman make her way toward them, and it didn't take a genius to see that she was disappointed. Maybe it was her mother's shorts that might have been a little too short. Maybe it was Mavis's wild tangle of hair that hadn't seen a comb since they'd left Hadley yesterday afternoon. Or maybe it was the smell of greasy food and bus fumes that swirled around the dreary bus station.

But whatever it was, it was clear that Mrs. Tully was struggling to make her mouth smile as her eyes darted from Mavis to her mother to the battered suitcases at their feet.

ROSE

The woman tugged on her shorts and thrust her hand toward Mrs. Tully. "I'm Luanne," she said.

Mrs. Tully set her mouth in a hard line and said, "*Mrs. Jeeter* seems more appropriate. I mean, under the circumstances."

"Well, okay, but it's *Miss* Jeeter."

Rose stood behind her mother, feeling shy, as usual. She wasn't very good at meeting new people, especially in front of her mother, who would always give her a nudge and tell her what to say. "For heaven's sake, Rose," she'd scold, "introduce yourself."

"Well, okay then, Miss Jeeter," Mrs. Tully said. "I hope your bus ride wasn't too bad." She gave her hair a pat and added, "I imagine those buses can be pretty horrid."

Miss Jeeter shrugged and said, "It's not like I haven't put in my time on a bus. But avoid the seats in the back, where the bathrooms are, if you know what I mean." She winked at Mrs. Tully, who cleared her throat and shifted her purse from one arm to the other.

And then, much to Rose's surprise, Miss Jeeter's wild-haired daughter came hopping over on one foot and said, "I'm Mavis. You be my best friend, okay?"

Rose looked around the bus station to see if there were any other kids there. Was this girl talking to *her*? Best friend? In all her ten years, she had never really had a best friend. Well, maybe one. Ida Scoggins. She had lived next door to the Tullys in Magnolia Estates when they first moved there. She had taught Rose how to make origami frogs and let Rose walk her dog named Frenchie, who wore a sweater and once bit Monroe Tucker, the gardener. She always made Rose laugh by doing the hula in the sprinkler or putting chopsticks in her nose. Then one day Ida had painted Rose's fingernails bright red. The name of the color was Va-Va-Voom, and Rose had loved it. But Mrs. Tully called Ida's mother, and after that, Ida didn't seem to want to play much anymore. And then the Scoggins moved to North Carolina, and that was the end of that.

And now it seemed like the other girls in Magnolia Estates only wanted to shop at the mall with Amanda Simm and weren't interested in playing cards with Mr. Duffy. So when Mavis Jeeter said, "You be my best friend, okay?" Rose felt a little wave of happiness work its way from her toes to the top of her head.

"Okay," she said, feeling her cheeks burn.

"Shall we go?" Mrs. Tully motioned toward the Jeeters' beat-up bags before heading for the door to the parking lot.

Miss Jeeter snatched up a duct-taped suitcase and followed her.

"Help me carry this," Mavis said to Rose, picking up one end of an overstuffed duffel bag.

Rose took the other end, and the girls hurried out to the parking lot.

Rose could hardly believe how good this day had turned out. Just yesterday she had spent the afternoon sitting alone on the porch between Pete and Larry, and now here she was carrying a duffel bag with her new best friend.

MAVIS

While Mavis's mother chattered away in the front seat, telling Mrs. Tully about taking French cooking lessons at the YWCA with her cousin Elmira, who was in a Toyota commercial, Mavis told Rose about all the places they'd lived.

"And one time, we lived in a condo in Atlanta that had a Jacuzzi in the bathroom," she said. "But the landlord got mad 'cause we had a dog."

"What'd you do?" Rose asked.

"Gave the dog to my uncle Jerry."

"Oh."

"Once we lived with this crazy lady named Trixie who saved everything," Mavis said. "Like used paper cups and empty soup cans."

"Really?"

"And one time we lived over a Chinese restaurant, and I got free fortune cookies."

Rose's eyes grew wide. "How many places have you lived?"

"A bunch. But I might go live with my dad someday."

"Where does he live?"

"In Tennessee with his mother." She leaned toward Rose and added, "She's kind of mean, so that's a problem."

"Your grandmother?"

Mavis nodded. "I was supposed to stay there all summer last year, but she made me leave early."

Mavis was surprised to see Rose suddenly look a little sad. It was their very first day together as best friends, and already Rose felt bad about Mavis's mean grandmother. That was a good sign.

As the Tullys' car made its way up the interstate, Mavis ran her hand over the soft leather seats. Then she took off her flip-flops and wiggled her toes in the thick black carpet under her feet. There wasn't a speck of dust or a single crumb on that carpet. When Mavis's mother drove her boyfriend Mickey's car, the floor was always littered with moldy french fries and dirty napkins and gravel from the driveway. But then, when the transmission had gone, her mother had left the car on the side of the road, which made Mickey mad as all get-out. He and her mother had hollered at each other, and two days later Mavis was packing her duffel bag again.

Before long, Mrs. Tully turned off the interstate and zigged and zagged until they reached a wrought-iron gate across the road and a sign that read MAGNOLIA ESTATES.

"This is where you live?" Mavis asked Rose.

Rose nodded.

"Why is there a gate?"

But Rose didn't answer. She was waving to a gray-haired, whiskery-faced man in a small brick gatehouse.

"Who's that?" Mavis asked.

"Mr. Duffy." Rose kept waving out the back window of the car as they drove into Magnolia Estates. "He's really sad," she said.

"How come?"

"His dog died."

Rose looked down at her hands in her lap, and Mavis thought she was going to cry.

"What happened?"

Rose looked up. "What do you mean?"

"What happened to his dog?"

"She just got old." Rose let out a little sigh. "Mr. Duffy used to do magic tricks and play his kazoo and stuff. But he doesn't anymore. He never even wants to play checkers."

"Then we'll cheer him up," Mavis said.

"I've been trying."

"What've you tried?"

"Well, I took him some blackberries. And I showed him a new card trick from a magic book I got at school."

Mavis let out a little *pfft*. "You gotta do more than *that*."

"Like what?"

"I'll think of something." Mavis poked Rose's arm and added, "Trust me."